HOPE UNBROKEN

UNVEILED SERIES
BOOK THREE

CRYSTAL WALTON

IMPACT EDITIONS LLC

Published by Impact Editions, LLC

Book Layout ©2013 BookDesignTemplates.com

Cover Design © 2020 Blue Water Books

Author Photo by Charity Mack

Hope Unbroken/Crystal Walton.

LCCN: 2015915849 (pbk.) | ISBN: 978-0-9862882-5-8 (pbk.) | ISBN 978-0-9862882-4-1 (eBook)

❀ Created with Vellum

PUMMELED

BREATHE. I unzipped my coat. A damp breeze rolled off the lake across from Riley's condo but didn't come close to lowering my body temperature. Not with the adrenaline still hanging on to my unanswered question.

Marry me tonight?

I hadn't planned to ask him that. Hadn't thought this through. I couldn't stay in Nashville. We both knew that. But now that I was here, nothing else mattered except being with him.

Riley didn't move. He kept one foot on the edge of the curb and one on the street, still frozen from bracing himself to hear what I'd come two thousand miles to say.

The uncertainty in his eyes deepened. "Emma, we're already engaged. I don't understand…"

Neither did I. Swallowing, I rubbed my hands on my jeans and glanced back at the blonde in the Honda parked along the curb. "I don't have any of this figured out. All I know is I'm ready now. We can—"

The sound of a car door slamming behind us sent a *clank* coursing down my already-tense body. Jake lifted his shaggy head from the grass, ears raised.

Riley's manager, Jessica, sashayed around the bumper. Each time her heels struck the concrete, my blood pressure ratcheted a little higher. No one should be allowed to make a pair of capris and fitted tee look that seductive.

She swept her long blond ponytail off her delicate shoulder as she approached us. "Nick called a meeting at eight," she said without so much as a glance in my direction.

Riley straightened. "It's Saturday."

"Your point?"

Rather than rise to her challenge, he simply held his ground. "I have other plans."

Jessica weaseled her phone out of her pocket and busied herself with the screen as though he hadn't spoken.

"Whatever it is, I'm sure it can wait. I'll call Nick—"

She whipped her head up. Patronizing smile in place, she strode two steps closer. "Considering your contract is the topic of conversation, I suggest you be there."

His contract?

Jake trotted over and nuzzled up beside Riley. Apparently, I wasn't the only one worried.

Jessica edged back, traded her cell for her keys, and widened her grin. "We can stop for breakfast first."

Riley's jaw flexed. "I'll meet you there."

She dipped her head in concession. "Just remember this is business. You don't have time for..." Her gaze slanted past him to me for the first time. "Distractions."

The accusation bulldozed straight through what little foundation was keeping my fatigued body standing.

Riley slipped an arm around my back and brought me close to his side.

Jessica turned to her car before he could get a retort out. Or maybe he knew it wasn't worth it. Either way, he steered me into his condo instead and whistled for Jake to follow.

The corners of his living room closed in on me again. His life was here—in contract meetings, rehearsals, performances. She was right. He couldn't afford any distractions.

I slumped against the couch arm. Maybe my coming wasn't the best thing for him. But how was I supposed to go back to Portland tonight with things unsettled? I'd come to fight for him, for us. If his contract kept him here even longer, where would that leave our plans?

Questions pummeled, stealing my certainty.

Until his eyes anchored me.

They didn't carry a shade of agitation left from the run-in with Jess, only assurance. "Em, you're the most important part of my life. You belong here."

Of course he knew what I was thinking. Despite what

else might have changed, that hadn't. And neither had his ability to calm my heart the way nothing else could.

Relief swept in, adrenaline waned, and pure exhaustion took hold of my body.

Riley caught my arm when I swayed. "I think it's about time you get some sleep." He led me to his bedroom. "Why don't you take a nap while I run to this quick meeting?"

Quick meeting? He made it sound like it was business as usual. He couldn't have missed the way Jess had taunted him like she was lording an ultimatum over him or something.

I stopped inside the doorway, torn in so many ways.

He traced the scar on my chin left from the night Tito attacked me outside my internship. "I know we have a lot to talk about, but you need to rest."

One look at my overtired reflection in the mirror left little room to argue.

I ran my fingers through my hair down to the grimy ends. "Actually, do you mind if I shower first?" The cab ride from the airport was enough to warrant a shower. Never mind that I'd been up for over twenty-four hours.

Riley struggled to keep the corners of his mouth in place. He grabbed an extra set of towels from a narrow closet in the bathroom and laid them on the sink counter along with my backpack. "Do you want me to leave something out for breakfast?"

I squinted to read the clock on his nightstand. 7:00

a.m. It would've passed as an acceptable time for breakfast if my stomach didn't beg to differ.

He laughed at my wrinkled nose as he shut the bathroom door.

Once alone, I cranked on the water, flexed both palms against the shower wall, and let the stress of everything leading up to today evaporate with the steam rising to the ceiling.

I didn't think anything could top that shower, but brushing my teeth had to be some small piece of heaven. In front of the sink, I dragged a hand towel across the mirror. A halfway normal version of myself was better than nothing. Hopefully, a nap would restore the rest.

I dug in my bag in search of my pajamas. After thirty seconds of not finding them, I dumped the whole thing out and rummaged through the clothes and toiletries strewn across the bathroom rug.

You've got to be kidding me.

Wrapped in a towel, I cracked the door. "Um, Riley? I was in such a rush to leave yesterday, I forgot to pack pajamas." *Like a complete idiot.* "Do you maybe have something I can borrow?"

Having the door almost completely closed should've at least diminished the reach of his boyish grin.

Without saying anything, he fished through two dresser drawers. His grin extended across the room and peaked to the left as he handed me a solid blue T-shirt and a pair of black mesh shorts.

I slid the clothes through the slender opening, threw

them on, and gave my hair a good wringing with the second towel. A single glimpse in the mirror was more than enough. The oversized clothes were almost as baggy as the skin under my eyes. And that tangled jumble of hair. Wow. Clearly, a nap was more in order than I'd thought.

Another peek around the edge of the door didn't show any sight of Riley. Maybe I'd caught a break this time. I hurried toward his bed.

"You look cute in my clothes."

I leaped a foot in the air.

Since when was a train wreck cute?

Riley lounged against the jamb with the corner of his lips hitched up his cheek. He'd freshened up from his run. Drops of water clung to the tips of hair hanging in a flawless mess over his forehead. Faint traces of his Nautica cologne curled around me and joined the same tender embrace his eyes offered mine.

He crossed the room and wove his hands around the small of my back. Being in his arms boxed out every other thought, rational or irrational. I twisted my wet hair over my shoulder and chewed on my lip and the question I knew I shouldn't ask. "Stay?"

"You keep looking that adorable, and I might not be able to say no."

That made two of us.

My cell rang from my purse on the bed. It was probably Jaycee, wondering if I'd made it here okay.

I swiped the screen. "Hey, I meant to call when I landed, but I got a little sidetracked."

"You don't say."

I looked over my shoulder. Yep, Riley's smile most definitely fit into the *sidetracking* category. Not that I had to spell it out to my best friend.

"Listen, I wouldn't have called, but I just ran into A. J., and..."

A. J.? My stomach clenched. "And what? What's wrong?"

"It's the center."

One jab followed another. My legs found the edge of the bed. Tito was in custody. He couldn't still be threatening the center. Had someone else taken over his gang? Someone looking for revenge? Tito had turned *himself* in for shooting Dee. They shouldn't blame us for that.

"I didn't get all the details," Jaycee said. "Something about a notice from the landlord."

I sank a palm onto the mattress, relief settling. Being behind on rent wasn't new news. We'd been working on a plan for months now. "I'm sure it's fine. Mr. Glyndon knows Trey is trying to—"

"I'm sorry, Em. The center's closing."

For the second time today, my breathing stopped.

2

UNCONDITIONAL

MY EYES FLUTTERED open to a sliver of warmth sprawling over my face. Despite the curtain's valiant effort to block it, the sun found a way to sneak its rays into the room. Not that I minded. Splashed in sunlight, I breathed in the scent of Riley's sheets and the contentment of being in his world.

Until I remembered.

The imprint left from Jaycee's phone call stripped away the dream-filled haze clouding my head. So much for a nap lessening the blow. It sank in all over again.

Trey couldn't run the center by himself and deal with this curveball too. I needed to get back to help. No question. But going meant leaving Riley, and I wasn't ready to—

Something wet rubbed against my hand. Jake's cold nose followed my arm up the mattress. I scratched him behind his ears. "No rest for the weary, huh?"

Head angled, he panted with gusto.

"I hear ya, buddy. Need to go out?"

He jumped in the air and bolted through the bedroom door.

"Guess that's a yes." I tossed off the covers, exchanged Riley's shorts for my jeans, and headed into the living room.

With another near backflip, Jake barked an urgent plea for me to let him out.

A chilled breeze pooled inside the second I opened the glass door. Jake cleared the stoop in a single gallop and set off on a mission to mark every inch of the backyard with his scent. *It's all yours, boy.*

Shuddering from the cold, I slid my feet into a warm pair of slippers beside the door and turned for the living room. I'd been too tired when I'd first arrived to notice much about the place. It held a different persona than Riley's Portland apartment, that was for sure.

The modern art's clashing colors were a far cry from his whitewashed walls back home. And the crimson microfiber couch looked more like something from a Pier 1 Imports display room than anything Riley would ever have picked out.

It was strange. He fit the music industry so well and yet still seemed out of place, as if passing through a pre-furnished hotel on a temporary visit. Maybe he hadn't fully moved on with his life as much as I'd thought.

I sat on the piano bench and chuckled at the number

of coffee cups congregated on top of the mantle. Some things never changed.

The edge of a picture poked out from behind the sheet music above the keys. I slipped it out the rest of the way to find a worn copy of one of my favorite photos of us at Reed. I smoothed the furled corners and traced the fingerprints left by Riley's hands. How many times had he looked at this?

"You're up," he said from the front door.

I swung around on the bench. "And you're late."

"Sorry. I stopped by the store on my way home." He swayed two grocery bags in the air. "Frozen-meal-in-a-bag. I wanted you to feel at home."

I strained to keep a straight face.

He laughed. "Yep, still adorable." After putting the food in the freezer, he joined me on the bench. His hair fell into his eyes as he pressed a shoulder into mine and nodded at the picture. "You got me through a lot of nights. Even when I didn't get to hear your voice, seeing your face was enough to keep me going."

His gaze followed mine toward the collection of mugs above us. "Well, you and coffee."

"Roadblock?"

"You could say that." With one collective swoop, he bunched the pages of sheet music into a single stack. "I've been having a rough time on this one song. But I think I might've finally broken through."

I studied him, searching for an explanation.

His eyes creased above a smile. "You have no idea, do you?"

"What?"

He shook his head, stretched his fingers over the keys, and let the piano's rich tenor fill in for his response. It didn't matter how many times I'd listened to his music— recorded and live, in dreams and in person. Nothing could lessen his ability to bind my heart to his when he played.

All the questions I'd asked, every trial we'd gone through, had been worth the price for him to be this close to his dreams. He couldn't lose them now.

I angled to face him and the uncertainty before us. "What happened at the meeting?"

He lowered his hands to his lap but kept his focus on the keys.

I swallowed, not sure I was ready for the answer.

He slid off the bench and handed me a coat twice my size. "C'mon, take a walk with me."

Why was he evading the question? Nerves pulsed. But once outside, snuggled next to him, I left the unanswered behind. The crisp wind intensified as we neared the lake across from his condo complex.

Riley covered my hand with his. "Emma, listen, about Jess—"

"You don't have to apologize. I shouldn't have jumped to conclusions. It was childish."

He stopped on the trail. "I'm not gonna pretend it didn't hurt to know you'd think I'd ever cheat on you, but I understand. Jess can be a little..." He lowered his chin and blew out a gruff breath. "...driven at times."

Was that what he called it?

His stare bored into the ground another minute before returning to me. "I feel like I owe you an explanation."

He started down the gravel again. I followed closely beside, torn between wanting to hear his voice and fearing what he had to say. As concerned as I was about the outcome of his meeting, talking about his relationship with Jessica might've been worse.

"She was a lifesaver when I first got here. Helped me get acclimated to the industry faster than I ever would've on my own. But after a while, it was clear she had... other intentions." His self-conscious laugh held a note of frustration. "As soon as I realized it, I set her straight."

I buried my coat cuffs under my fingers. "What'd you say?"

"That I was already engaged." He shrugged like there were no ifs, ands, or buts about it. "I told her I drew a hard, fast line she couldn't cross if she wanted to stay my manager."

I fell a step behind. "How'd she take it?"

"As well as she takes anything." He rubbed the back of his hair in snappy flicks. "She kept trying to inch past that line. The day she answered my phone when you called, that was it. I had enough. It took a few days before I could even handle talking to her."

Riley kicked a loose rock into the lake. "I told her I'd

honor the work she's contributed to the album. But after it's released, we're done."

A mixture of pride and respect for him collided with my own feelings of deficiency and failure for not drawing clearer lines with A. J.

I stopped again, this time lagging several paces behind. "I just want you to know that nothing ever happened between A. J. and me. We got too close emotionally, but it was never more than that."

Riley enclosed me in his arms. If he held any resentment, he didn't show it. He laced his fingers through mine. "Can I take you somewhere?"

He barely waited for me to nod before whisking me off the trail. He pointed to street vendors and corner shops while narrating parts of his daily routine—favorite sandwich joints, cafés with the best teas he'd tried out just for me, notorious spots to hear live music.

The fiercer the wind blew, the tighter I nestled against Riley's woolen coat. But getting to share in these little moments with him kept me warmer than anything else.

He slowed in front of a two-story brick building. The unwavering smile that had led us here expanded as he unlocked the glass door. "Ready?"

I crossed the threshold into a space that looked much like the entryway of any office building, minus the records framed on the walls.

He grabbed my hand and tugged me toward a staircase. "This way."

On the second floor, he strolled over to a metal desk beside a window facing the street and withdrew a set of keys from the middle drawer. "You're gonna love—"

Riley jerked a glance toward the sound of footsteps funneling up the narrow stairway.

Jess rounded the corner, looking like she'd just stepped off the set of some provocative legal drama. Her moment's surprise at seeing us dimmed behind a smirk as she traipsed in.

I lifted my chin but gripped the desk at the same time.

She was everything I wasn't—a walking personification of all my insecurities. Sleek and shiny, her calves glistened in the light. She'd traded her capris and tee for a black pencil skirt accentuating her nonexistent waistline and a satiny dress shirt that appeared to be missing the two most important buttons.

Though her gaze never retracted from Riley, the rest of her movement flowed with the graceful poise of a runway model. A foot away, she hurled a blatant once-over down my body from head to toe.

Riley draped an arm around me. "I don't believe you've officially met Emma. My fiancée," he added with a note of satisfaction.

The introduction probably called for a customary handshake, but neither of us breached the impasse.

Her scrutiny burned with calculated force before she dismissed my presence altogether. Again. A flick of her lashes returned her focus to Riley. "I was just coming in to grab some paperwork." She brushed against his body while leaning over the desk. "See you Monday." Her perfectly straight hair fanned over her shoulders as she turned. "Oh," she said a few feet away. "Have you told her yet?"

I looked at Riley. "Told me what?"

Jess flaunted a grin that clearly relished my response. "Guess not."

A tendon on his neck twitched. "Nick wants me to start touring in February."

"So soon?"

"He's working on landing me an opening slot for another artist in a push to get some singles out."

"How long will you tour?"

Riley's jaw twitched like it was trying to change the answer. "A year," he said softly.

A year? I tried to restrain the disappointment clawing up my chest before it reached my face. It'd be okay. These last four months apart had been painful, but I had to believe that we'd come out stronger. We'd figure this out too.

He turned toward me, barricading Jess out of view. "Don't worry. I already told Nick it's going to have to wait until after you graduate and we get married."

"What? Riley, no—"

Jess clicked her tongue. "Aw, you're leaving out the best part."

It took everything in me not to choke her little singsong voice.

Riley glared at her. "Don't you have somewhere to be?"

"Come to think of it, I have a road trip to plan." Her smug tone flittered across the room and joined another overhauling glare right before she vanished down the stairs.

He shook his head. "Sorry about that. Just ignore her."

Not going to happen. "What's she talking about, the best part? What's going on?"

He loosened his grip around the keys and headed toward a side room. "She likes to exaggerate. It's just some fine print stuff I'm working out with Nick. It's nothing to worry about." He flipped on the lights to the studio. "C'mon, I want to show you where I've been recording all semester."

One step through a door shouldn't have been able to neutralize the nervous energy still surging on the other side of it, but something about the studio overrode everything except being swept into Riley's dreams. From the soundboards lining the walls to the stool behind a screened microphone in the middle of the curved room, this was where he thrived.

I turned, not knowing what to say. Closer than expected, he met my eyes right before my lips. My back pressed into the doorframe.

His grin toppled sideways when he finally released me. "Just in case you were starting to doubt my feelings for you."

As if his smile would ever let me. Jess might've gotten

away with causing me to question Riley's commitment once. Not again.

He motioned inside. "C'mon."

At the stool, he strapped on his guitar and began a song as he would've for a live recording. He pulled me next to him. "Your turn."

My blank stare drifted to the microphone. "You kidding me?"

"Hang on." He jogged out and reappeared behind the window separating the studio and the control room. After fiddling with the equipment for a minute, he pointed at a headset resting on top of the music stand.

He *was* serious. I lugged on the headphones, and background music filled my ears.

Riley materialized beside me again. He lifted one side of the headset and handed me sheet music so I could follow along as he sang.

I picked up the chorus, singing in a whisper until he caught me. He angled the microphone closer to my mouth.

"Riley..."

He cocked his head. "I'm not making you nervous, am I?"

With my lips pinched together, I shook my head. "Only until I close my eyes."

Like the first time I'd played my guitar for him, I hid behind my eyelids and let the music take over. By the second time through, I held nothing back.

I opened my eyes, expecting to see Riley's satisfied

face beaming at me, but he'd disappeared behind the window again, busy mastering the mixing console.

He hunched over a small microphone. "Keep singing like that, and you might end up on my album."

The sheet music dropped from my hand to the floor. I yanked off the headphones. "You wouldn't." I scampered out of the room. "Riley!"

We collided around the corner, caught up in a moment as if no time had passed since last summer. But when the sunset tapered, it didn't take long for an unbidden sense of gravity to replace our laughter with the reminder that our time was running out.

I clutched my elbows across my chest. How was I supposed to say goodbye to him again?

Somehow knowing, Riley enveloped me in his arms and in a look mirroring the words neither of us said.

He locked up the studio and returned the keys to the drawer while I meandered around the space that held his future.

"Ready?" he said.

Hardly.

He kept me close to his side on the walk back. After failing to win him over with my frozen-meal-in-a-bag dinner, we drank the teas we'd picked up at a corner café and talked until a honk from outside his condo signaled the end of my visit.

The streetlamp glared over the yellow taxi parked at the curb. Riley set my bag on the back seat and paid the cabdriver, who—thankfully—didn't look nearly as sketchy as the one who'd dropped me off yesterday.

Not that I wanted to get into *any* cab. Period.

Riley mimicked my frown. "I don't want you to leave any more than you do, but you have to get back for finals."

Why couldn't we have graduated at the same time?

I toyed with the hem of his shirt. "You *sure* you don't want to elope?"

He edged closer. "Don't tempt me."

We could tease about it all we wanted, but time apparently had its own plans, as usual.

Riley gently turned my chin toward his.

I brought his thumb to my lips. "I love you."

His smile said the same. "Always."

The cab driver leaned through the window, held his hand out in front of his face, and made googly eyes at it. "No, I love *you* more," he said in a lovey-dovey voice.

His impersonation cracked us up and earned him an extra tip for instigating some much-needed levity.

"Meter's running," he said as he rolled up the window.

Riley kissed the top of my head. "I should be back by winter break."

At least he had off for the holidays. I still sensed there was more to that meeting than he was letting on. The way Jess had alluded to whatever the "best part" was made it sound too much like his contract was on the line.

Forcing down my selfishness, I looked up at him. As

much as I wanted to marry him right now, I'd wait. "Riley, touring is important. If Nick thinks you should start in February, you should."

He drew in a breath. "There are more important things than touring… Things I've actually been meaning to talk to you about." The engine's hum almost drowned out his voice.

My muscles tensed.

He scuffed his sneaker along the curb and stared at the ground. "Em, there's something I need you to do for me."

3

WHIRLWIND

GO HOME to meet the family Riley had been estranged from for how many years? The ones who didn't even know I existed? Sure, just show up on their doorstep on Christmas Eve. Why not? I pressed the heel of my hand to my forehead. What was he thinking?

Mulling over Riley's request had kept me awake for most of the red-eye flight. I hiked my book bag strap up to the top of my shoulder while the moving runway escorted me farther along the airport corridor. With my lack of sleep piling up on me, maybe this wasn't the best time to think about it. Being back in Portland brought on enough pressures to deal with on its own—finals, A. J., the center.

I let out a long breath. One hurdle at a time.

Thankfully, I didn't have to go through it all alone. Jaycee flagged me down from the opposite end of the terminal. She squeezed me so hard, you'd think we hadn't seen each other in months rather than mere hours.

She lifted my left hand for inspection before saying anything else. "No wedding band?"

Of course she knew I ended up asking him to elope.

"Don't worry, Jae. I'd never deprive you of getting to plan my wedding day."

She tossed an arm around my shoulders and steered me toward the exit. "Liar."

Our laughter echoed off the vaulted ceiling as we spun through the circular doors into a misty December morning.

A look of intrigue built behind her eyes. I couldn't even hint at the prospect of wedding planning without sparking a chain of ideas. For her sake, I was glad Riley hadn't taken me up on my impulsive suggestion to go to Vegas. Strange how long ago that conversation seemed now.

At her Fiat, I opened my door and studied her across the hood. "It didn't even cross your mind to check if there was still an engagement ring on my finger, did it?"

She lounged her forearm along the doorframe, angled her head, and stared at me like I'd asked a no-brainer. "Of course not."

I buckled in as she cranked the heat. A blast of tropical air freshener clashed with the coffee scent forever embedded in her car's upholstery.

Several miles down the road, I tore my gaze away

HOPE UNBROKEN | 23

from the flashes of scenery passing by us. "You're not going to ask me what happened?"

"Wasn't sure you were ready to talk about it."

I towed my legs up into the seat and rested my chin on my knees, still sorting through it all myself. "Can everything and nothing change at the same time? It's weird. In some ways, I feel like we're in a new relationship. Like, we've reached this place we hadn't been able to before. But it also seems like we picked things up right where we left off in August."

I dragged my finger down the condensation on the window. "Guess it sounds sort of crazy."

"It sounds like love," Jaycee said. "You grow. You change. That's part of life. Doing it *together* is what makes love work."

I seriously needed to check for some kind of shared transmitter between her and my brother.

She glanced at my expression. "What?"

"The musings of Jaycee McAllister."

She yanked off her glove with her teeth and flung it at me.

I doubled over. She might've been a lot like Austin, but there were some roles only a best friend could fill. No chance I would've survived college without her. She was right. Again. Riley and I'd both changed, but we were in this together. I shoved down my worry about whatever Nick and Jess were lording over him. Now that I was back, the center needed my focus.

Jaycee parked in front of our campus apartment.

Outside, I inhaled Reed College's familiar aroma of ever-greens and exhaled the residual stress left from my whirlwind weekend. I took out my cell and jutted my chin at the door. "I'll be up in a minute."

She trekked into the stairwell, and I backed against the fender.

Trey answered my call on the first ring. "You heard."

No beating around the bush. "Yeah, secondhand. Why didn't you call me?"

"Aw, now, there was no use interfering with your trip."

Was he serious? Every minute counted. If Dee's death hadn't taught us that much, nothing would've. He'd come so far—from a broken gang member to a boy who hoped for a new future. Dee had lost his chance too soon. I wouldn't let that be in vain.

"Well, I'm back, and I'm coming in tomorrow."

"Emma, I've already turned in your performance review. It's the last few weeks of the semester. Why don't you focus on your studies?"

Background noise from the center swept in with sounds tied to my heart. It wasn't only an internship. It was a part of me. "You know where I stand, Trey."

His husky laugh trickled through the line. "Didn't leave your stubbornness in Nashville, huh?"

"It's not stubbornness." I lifted off the car and smoothed out my coat. "It's perspective. This wise sage once told me keeping perspective is the only way to make it through life."

His laughter mushroomed. "I'll be sure to try that," he said, repeating the same thing I'd said when he'd tried that adage on me months ago.

Bass from a passing car rocked into the stillness. "I just don't want to see you get hurt."

He couldn't be giving up already. Quitting wasn't in his DNA. There had to be more to the story. "What aren't you telling me?"

The commotion in the background died down. He must've stepped outside. "Three months, Emma. That's all we have left."

4

UNFINISHED

A NIGHT in my own bed hadn't released the strain in my shoulders the way it should've. I shut my car door, massaged the crook of my neck, and faced the brick building that had been a second home for me this last semester. There had to be a way to keep the center open. It meant too much.

I cast a glance down both sides of the street. A BMW with tinted windows sat a block away between two beat-up clunkers, looking like a shiny silver dollar in a pile of grungy pennies. I almost headed over to check if the driver was lost but sensed I shouldn't.

Noise coming from the opposite end of the road turned me toward the empty street corner. A chill in the wind climbed up my neck. I willed back the wave of uneasiness. It was broad daylight for Pete's sake.

Apparently, my feet didn't care. They hurried me across the street until a ring from my cell stopped me short. In the middle of the road, I stared at the unknown number.

My back stiffened at the sound of rustling coming from behind me. Without answering the call, I picked up my pace.

An eerie whistle sailed toward me. Heavy footsteps followed. Dark memories from the night Tito had attacked me on this same corner cropped up without warning.

Clutching my purse strap, I skirted around the building, yanked open my purse, and wrangled out the pepper spray Trey had made me swear to keep on hand. I clasped it with two sweaty palms.

The footsteps drew nearer, the whistle louder. *Breathe.* Pepper spray at the ready, I pushed off the wall at the same time a hefty man in a ball cap rounded the corner.

He dropped whatever he'd been carrying. "Whoa." He tugged on his earphones and raised his hands. "Easy, miss."

"Who are you?" I kept my finger on the trigger.

He didn't move. "My name's Max. Just doing my job."

The BMW squealed past us and stirred up a cloud of burnt rubber and exhaust.

I flicked my chin at him. "What job?"

He directed my eyes toward the ground before bending down in slow motion. With continued caution, he picked up the paper, eased back to his feet, and held it out to me.

A "For Rent" sign?

He lowered his arms when I finally lowered the spray. "Sorry, miss. I gotta post this on your door. Then I'll be outta your way."

"But we still have three months." Didn't we?

He shrugged. "Just following orders."

I'd like to tell him what he could do with his orders.

I followed beside him, still gripping my spray can. Something felt... off. He jimmied a roll of tape from his pocket as I stalled by the door.

"Who was in that silver BMW?"

He tore off a piece of tape with his teeth. "What BMW?"

"You didn't notice that peel out a minute ago?"

He hung the roll on his wrist and leveled out the sign. "Figured it was some kids."

"In a beamer?"

"Didn't get a good look at the car. Just heard 'em tires." He secured the sign with a final piece of tape and dusted off his hands, as if he'd finished a day's hard work. "Alrighty, that'll do it." He tipped his hat at me and turned.

Adrenaline still pulsing, I jetted inside and left the door open.

Trey met my eyes from his desk, already knowing.

I pointed at the sign anyway. "Did you know he was doing this?"

His glance circled by Darius and Brandon on its way

back to me. "Mr. Glyndon told me he was sending someone by."

"And you just let him?" Trey had always been able to work things out with our landlord. I didn't understand.

He adjusted his dark-rimmed glasses. "I'm not exactly in a position to argue."

How could he say that? If we didn't rally for the center, who would?

He motioned to Darius. "Give a holler to the guys out back, will ya? Tell them it's time to hit the books."

Darius corralled his peers off the basketball court and led them into the classroom. After all that time being A. J.'s right-hand man on the court, he'd earned a certain respect from the rest of the kids.

I charged straight for my desk phone and the chance to give Mr. Glyndon an earful. Only one ring went through before his voicemail kicked in.

Trey eased the receiver from my ear and set it in its base. "I broke the lease, Emma. We're four months behind on rent. He's doing what he needs to."

"But he was working with us. What changed?"

"Not sure." He tucked one arm under the other. "It's business. Guess grace wore out its welcome. At least he gave us three months' notice."

Like that made any difference. I slouched in my chair. "Can we move somewhere else?"

His forehead creased. "No one's gonna sign a lease with someone who can't even pay a deposit, let alone keep up with rent. Mr. Glyndon owns half the city's buildings, anyway, and rubs shoulders with whoever owns the rest."

I booted up my computer. "Why couldn't the Success Foundation have sent someone other than Mr. Brake? We wouldn't even be in this situation if he hadn't blown our chance at getting that grant."

"But we are." Trey squeezed my shoulder and brandished one of his famous father looks. "No use casting blame."

"Sorry. It's just frustrating."

"I know." He smiled with the same assurance that had guided his actions time and again. "It's gonna be okay."

Breathing in, I nodded.

He waved a hand over the mess that was supposed to be my desk. "We missed you while you were away."

"I see that."

His laugh boosted my spirits. Rent sign up or not, we were still here, which meant it was time to get to work. He strolled off to the classroom, and I dove in.

I shuffled the bills into a giant pile and glanced at the trash can. Tempting. I shoved them into my inbox instead to deal with later. Right now, finding funding was the only thing I needed to tackle.

I pulled up Google. Were there any grant leads left? Even if there were, three months wouldn't be enough time to pull it all together. I raked my hair out of my face. If Mr. Brake hadn't flown off the handle, we'd already have the funds we needed. His arrogance still burned me. The assumptions he'd made. How he'd accused Dee of things he didn't have anything to do with and then wrote us off like we were nothing. The whole thing made me want to scream.

A wave of young voices rolled out from the classroom and settled over me in a plea to focus on the present instead of the past.

I opened my notebook to a clean page, tapped my pen against the desk, and drew another deep breath. I had to try.

After hours of scouring sites for a possible benefactor and catching up on my regular work, I stashed my pen into the notebook's spiral binding and sank into the back of my chair.

Trey passed my desk on his way to his own. His gaze skimmed my scribbled notes, but he didn't mention it. "Is Riley living it up in Nashville like I told him?"

I returned his grin. "Just for you."

"Knew he'd come through for me." He bottomed into his chair and tilted back with his hands laced behind his head. "Ahh... the vicarious life. That's how we old folks roll."

Would there ever be a time he couldn't make me laugh?

"How do you do it, Trey?"

He lowered his glasses down his nose and dished out an expression that said "perspective" without any words necessary.

The back screen door shuddered into its frame as little Andre shuffled over to Trey's desk. He craned his head and scanned the office, face falling. "No Mr. A. J. again?"

My heart winced.

"Not today, buddy." Trey rolled his chair around his desk and held out a hand. "How 'bout we keep up that secret handshake for when he comes back."

Andre's chin scuffed the tattered collar of his beat-up Nike sweatshirt as he swayed his head. "It's not the same."

Nothing was.

Trey kept his hand out, not missing a beat. "Aw, c'mon. You're the big dawg around here now. I'm counting on you to school me."

A teeny smile crept up Andre's chubby cheeks. "A'ight." He clasped Trey's hand and showed him how he and A. J. used to do it.

Andre whipped around toward a holler from the basketball court and scurried outside.

Though frayed on all accounts, the court still offered them a home. It did for all of us—A. J. included. He should've been here. Especially now, when Trey needed help more than ever.

I leaned on my elbows and held my head in both hands. "I'm sorry, Trey. About A. J. not being here. It's my fault."

Trey's chair squeaked into an upright position. He crossed his arms over his desk. "Now, don't you go blaming yourself for that. And don't worry about A. J., either. He'll be back. Give him some time."

I ran my finger along the dust-filled crease on my keyboard. "I'm not so sure about that."

A smile curved under his scruffy mustache. He moseyed to the back door and leaned one heavy shoulder against the jamb. "The kids stirred him while he was here. That doesn't just go away. Believe me, I know."

So did I.

"I hope you're right."

"I usually am. Another of those old folks' perks." He fake-stumbled across the room, trying to keep a straight face while hunching over like an elderly person.

He might've been pushing fifty, tops. Even younger in spirit. But there was no denying the business side of things had aged him. My chest deflated at the thought.

At his desk, Trey settled onto his chair and kneaded out the imprint of another long week from his shoulders. His gaze shifted with his tone. "You should visit him."

Holding a pile of papers together, I tugged open the center drawer to grab a paperclip. "I don't think A. J. wants to see me."

"I wasn't talking about A. J." He angled his chin when my glance caught his. "I was referring to Tito."

The papers skimmed the inside of my hand and hit the floor. The air in the room vanished. I couldn't hear the name of the person responsible for Dee's death without anger constricting my chest until I couldn't breathe.

I dropped to my knees, shoved the loose pages into a disheveled pile, and fought back the wave. "Tito's in jail." Where he belonged.

Trey hiked up a brow. "They have this thing called visiting hours."

I sat back on my heels. "You can't be serious? Why in the world would I want to visit *him?*"

"Because you have unfinished business with *him.*"

I towed myself back up to my chair and straightened the papers from every possible angle. "I don't know what you're talking about."

I didn't have to meet his eyes to tell he didn't buy it.

"If you leave that bitterness festering, Tito won't be the only one imprisoned."

I stared past him into the memory of the day Dee had first told me about his artwork. The chains of self-doubt that had bound him left permanent marks on my heart the same way the look on Tito's face the day I'd confronted him had left permanent scars.

I choked down the emotion and looked away. Knowing what Trey was saying didn't make it any easier to swallow. "I don't think I'm ready."

Rather than press further, he made his way over to my desk. "It's been a long day." He dipped his head toward the door. "Let me walk you to your car."

A quick glance at the clock announced my shift had ended ten minutes ago.

I tossed a couple of far-reaching grant requests into the outgoing mailbox, tied my scarf around my neck, and flung on my coat. It *had* been a long day, but I couldn't call it quits yet. "Trey?" I asked on our way outside. "Do you think Dee's mom would let me get my hands on some of his artwork? I want to see about getting it printed."

A shade of sadness colored his eyes. "I think Dee would've been honored."

I tucked the sides of my coat over my stomach and curbed back the sense of loss we both wrestled.

The afternoon sunlight reflecting off neighboring buildings defied the chilled air whirling around us.

Trey stopped in front of Riley's car and stared at the pavement. "I don't see much of Ms. Mendierez anymore. Sorry to say, I hear she drinks much of her life away these days." He rested a hand on my shoulder. "You can stop by her house, Emma, but don't expect much of a reception."

I swallowed at the heaviness in his eyes.

In the driver's seat, I snapped on my seat belt and faced the road leading to a conversation I wasn't even sure how to start.

A succession of one-way streets brought me to Dee's home. The car idled in front of the mailbox. With my hands clenched around the steering wheel, I peered back and forth between the run-down townhouse and the street. Did she still live here? Would she even want to talk to me? What if she was an angry drunk? Maybe this was a bad idea.

I grabbed the gearshift, ready to hightail it out of

there, until a shriek rang from the house. Something in me sparked. Without hesitation, I raced up the walkway to the faded blue door. Locked. A *clank* banged inside like someone was trashing the place.

My pulse picked up. Not knowing what else to do, I crouched around the window. I couldn't see through the opaque glass, but the heavy-scented gust of alcohol seeping through the crack must've meant one thing.

Ms. Mendierez was home.

5

UNMOVING

THE MEMORY of Dee's face drew me to a stop halfway back to the car. He'd want me to be courageous. Not only for the kids in this neighborhood, but for his mom too.

A deep exhale collected in the cold air. I turned and marched back to the door. "Ms. Mendierez?" I called. "It's Emma. Emma Matthews... from the center. We met last week."

Noise rattled behind the door, but it didn't budge.

"I was a friend of Dee's." I held my breath, praying the mention of her belated son wouldn't make things worse.

The front door creaked open. A distorted replica of the confident woman I'd met at the center peered from inside. Her hair was matted down from every angle like she hadn't showered in days. Deep circles under her eyes matched the door she was clutching to keep from tumbling over.

"Yes?"

"Ms. Mendierez? I'm Emma. We met—"

"I remember." Her voice sounded pained, distant.

I had trouble finding my own. "Would you mind if I came inside for a minute?"

Her gaze wandered over her shoulder.

Maybe I should've at least called first. Given her some kind of warning. "If it's a bad time, I understand."

Shoulders dropping, she staggered backward and tied a loose belt strap around a gray, tattered bathrobe. The door swayed open and released another gust of alcohol-infused air from inside. This time, a mixed odor of soured laundry and stale take-out joined it.

Inside, I glanced into the living room from the entryway. A collection of drained liquor bottles cluttered a coffee table piled with papers and clothes overflowing onto the couch.

She stumbled into the hollow doorway between the two rooms to obstruct my view. "What can I do for you, Miss Matthews?" she slurred.

I backed up in search of the reason I'd come. "Um, actually, it's about Dee."

She hugged her arms to her stomach and stared right through me into memories I didn't need to see to feel. The disheveled place carried enough brokenness of its own.

Was there any way to restore what had been lost? I paced across the small entryway. "Your son was a very gifted artist. I was hoping—"

A rueful laugh caught me short. I looked up. "Ms. Mendierez?"

"I never even knew my boy liked to draw." Her face contorted with pain. "I found a sketchbook in his desk after..."

Compassion drew me toward her. "I think Dee was very self-conscious about it. He didn't realize how talented he was."

Her glassy eyes stayed locked on the wall.

I reached for her hand. "I think we have a good chance of getting his artwork printed. Maybe even selling some. My brother has connections. I came to ask if you'd be okay with us trying. Dee'd probably be embarrassed, but I think it would've made him happy."

For the first time since I'd arrived, a genuine smile graced her face. "Yes," she said. "Yes, I think you're right. It'd make him happy."

She motioned for me to go ahead of her up a worn staircase. Daylight dimmed behind us once we reached the top. Ms. Mendierez nudged me toward a bedroom door on the right.

I paused with my hand on the knob, unsure if I should go in. She didn't move from the top of the stairwell, only gestured for me to enter alone.

A door had never felt so heavy. The glare from a window on the opposite wall flooded the darkened hallway as I inched inside. The room looked like she'd left it exactly the way it'd been the last night Dee was there—rumpled covers balled up at the bottom of his bed, an untouched pile of dirty clothes hanging down the side of an open hamper, textbooks strewn across a small desktop.

My feet might as well have had weights tied to them. Surrounded by memories torn between what was and what would never be, I couldn't blame Ms. Mendierez for keeping his door closed.

I reached over an old wooden chair in front of his desk and picked up a black picture frame. An ear-to-ear smile radiated from an elementary-aged image of Dee, who had his arms wrapped around a man's broad shoulders. Based on the resemblance, it must've been his father.

Despite the damage his dad's abandonment had created, Dee's eyes didn't hold a drop of bitterness. Only grace.

"He loved that fool."

Ms. Mendierez's frail silhouette lined the doorframe, as though an invisible barrier prevented her from stepping into the room where even breathing felt unbearable.

"Damian ran off before Dee was out of training pants." That same dark laugh from earlier shadowed her words. "Oh, he'd show his face whenever he needed somethin'. Even put on a show like he cared 'bout spending time with his son. But it always ended the same. Always empty words. Same empty promises. He never had to see the look in Dee's eyes the next day." Lines of resentment burrowed into the creases on her forehead.

She stared absently at the picture in my hands and laughed lighter this time. "No matter what Damian did, that boy of mine loved his father something fierce. I'll never understand it."

Me neither. Even now, Dee was still teaching me what it meant to live with the kind of hope and courage no circumstance could shake.

I set the picture frame back on his desk and pointed to the center drawer. "May I?"

She nodded.

I only had to sift through a few loose papers to find the sketchpad Dee had shown me months earlier. Removing it uncovered a small brown leather journal. I peered at Ms. Mendierez again for permission.

She backed into the hallway. "Take your time."

The tremor in my hands kept me from opening the journal's worn binding all the way. This was part of Dee. A part I wasn't so sure I could handle seeing. But a name caught my eye before I closed it. I scanned backward until I found the beginning of the sentence: *I never blamed A. J. for his reaction when I first came to the center.*

I flipped the page over to the beginning of that day's entry. He'd written it only a couple of days before he died. I sank onto the chair as the memory of Dee's voice lifted off the page.

I wonder if this is what it's like to have a brother. Someone who cares about me enough to teach me when to man up to my potential. To show me how to treat a girl and live without holding anything back.

I never blamed A. J. for his reaction when I first came to the center. He saw what everyone else saw. But when he accepted me—even after he knew the things I'd done and was capable of doing—that didn't make no sense.

Guess it sounds crazy to think God would've gone to so much trouble to get me to the center just so I'd understand what it means to have a family. But what if he did? For the first time, I know what it feels like to walk through life with a brother by my side.

I wiped off the tears collected at the bottom of my chin. Did A. J. have any idea what kind of impact he'd made on Dee's life? He needed to read this. For Dee and for all the kids at the center, A. J. had to know what he'd be forfeiting if he didn't come back.

After one last scan around the room, I closed the door to the visible reminder of what we'd lost. But with the treasures Dee had left behind in my hands, I left knowing I'd do whatever it took to see his artwork printed.

"Ms. Mendierez?" I called when I reached the bottom of the steps.

Not a single sound.

I crept around the banister and followed a slender hallway into the kitchen. She sat at the table with a look of detachment glossing her eyes. A half-empty bottle of Bacardi weighed her arm to the floor beside shards of broken tumblers.

I stepped into her line of sight and raised the pad and journal. "If it's okay, I'd like to borrow these two things for a little while. I promise to return them just as they are."

She didn't stir. Didn't speak.

"If this is too much, I can—"

"It's fine, Miss Matthews." With a forced blink, she veered her focus toward me. The simple motion took longer than it should have.

Midway in a turn toward the door, I stopped. I couldn't leave. Not yet. I knelt by her side, pried the bottle from her cold hand, and held on.

"I know this is difficult to hear, and the last thing I want to do is be insensitive to what you're going through, but I can't leave without saying this." After how many times I'd needed people to speak hard truths into my life, it only seemed right for me to do the same for someone else.

"I won't pretend to understand what you're experiencing right now, but I know what it's like to lose a family member. To want to stay in bed instead of facing another day of unanswered questions." I sat back on my feet.

"But someone Dee loved very much had to remind me that giving up would only be dishonoring his memory." I squeezed her hand. "For Dee, please. Please don't stop living."

Her eyes softened but didn't release the fear of what returning to the present might cost. As much as I wanted to help her, she had to make the choice herself. I set her hand on her lap and pushed up on my thighs.

At the front door, I stalled one last time before closing it. The sunlit warmth soaked through my coat onto my back. What would it take to penetrate her walls?

A group of elementary kids raced toward a rundown playground while a city transit bus picked up a handful of people most likely headed into evening shifts.

Surrounded by the day's evidence that life carried on, I listened for any sign of Ms. Mendierez joining it, but none came. Not even a hint of motion.

Unmoving. I'd been there. Lived through it. But maybe it wasn't my place to influence her. Maybe it was Dee's. Even though he was gone, I had to believe his legacy would continue to impact those he left behind... including A. J.

6

CONSEQUENCES

I'D DONE my best to stay occupied and keep my mind off the helplessness that yesterday had stirred. But after cramming for finals all day, I needed a break.

The coffee fumes taking over the living room swallowed up my tea's spicy aroma. It was two cups against one. Not to mention Jaycee and Trevor's mugs were almost double the size of mine.

Trev tossed a throw pillow in the air above his head like he would a basketball. "So, what do you two want to do tonight?"

He'd probably asked that same question a couple hundred times over the last three and a half years. We were best friends. We hung out together all the time. But something about hearing him say *"you two"* wrought an unavoidable reminder of who was missing tonight.

A. J. wasn't busy with other plans or out of town. I'd

lost him. Things would be different now. They had to be different.

Trevor caught the pillow midair and appraised the look on my face. "What's wrong?"

"How is he?"

"A. J.?" Trev glanced at Jaycee, hesitating. "To be honest, I haven't seen much of him. He's pretty much been living in the gym, self-medicating."

Jaycee thrust an elbow shot to his ribs.

He doubled over. "What was that for? We all know Em broke his heart."

Jaycee gear-wrenched a hand around his forearm. "Trev!"

"No, he's right," I said. "There's no reason to pretend I haven't hurt him."

She tilted her head at me. "He'll be okay. Just—"

"Give it time. I know." My shoulders caved with doubt. I didn't want to argue, but she was wrong. Time, yet again, was the enemy.

Thoughts overlapped until I knew what I needed to do.

I scooted to the edge of the couch and ran my fingers along my mug handle. "Listen, you two go out and do something fun tonight. I'm going to stay behind this time."

Jaycee darted her head in my direction. Her angled bangs swooped across her eyes, but not before laser beams of warning streamed at me.

"Don't worry," I said. "No sinking back into depression. Promise. I have something I need to take care of. You guys go on. Really."

Trevor towed Jaycee up from the couch when she didn't budge. She dragged her feet across the carpet and stared at me over her shoulder until the door closed behind them.

I unfolded the piece of paper I'd photocopied from Dee's journal and reread it twice in hopes he would transfer his courage to me one more time. Ready or not, I threw on a coat and headed to the gym toward the confrontation waiting for me there.

A quick scan across the empty basketball courts led me downstairs toward the weight room. Weights clicked together and sent a sharp echo through the hall straight into the clatter already pounding against my rib cage.

I stopped outside the doorway. Seeing A. J. alone—basketball shorts, favorite red hoodie, ball cap on backward, like always—almost turned me right back around.

His gaze flickered to my reflection in the mirrored wall. A faint smile touched his eyes. "I had a feeling you'd come down here eventually."

His voice was as real and open as it had always been. I looked away before he saw how much I hated having to let go of that sound. "I'm sorry. I know I have no right to come—"

"Is that why you came? To apologize?" The dumbbells clanked into the rack and raised my shoulders even higher. "To apologize for what exactly?" He faced me.

"For all we went through together? Because I'm not sorry. For any of it."

Head down, I folded the corner of the paper in my hands back and forth. "A. J., I—"

"I know." He peeled open the Velcro straps on his gloves. "Riley's already won that battle."

"It's not a battle."

He tossed his gloves over his gym bag in the corner and smiled at my reflection in the mirror again. "Still naive."

A pang of defensiveness rose inside me, but the truth weighed it back down. The gravity of what my naiveté had cost us both filled the tiny room.

I stared at the black and white tiled floor. "You're right. I *was* naive. I thought we could just be friends. Thought we could be close without..."

"Without what?" He edged closer. "Letting me into your heart?"

The intensity in his brown eyes withered my voice to a whisper. "You're my friend, A. J. Of course you hold a place in my heart." Even if it was one neither of us could visit again.

The familiar grin I'd leaned on too much this past semester slanted to the left. "You know that's not what I meant."

Though he was standing directly in front of me now, I couldn't bring myself to meet his eyes. I untwisted the paper, but the knot in my chest kept tightening.

"I'm not saying I won't move on." He inched close

enough to hear my soft inhale. "But no amount of time will ever take away what I've experienced with you. Those memories aren't replaceable."

A. J. bent forward and lowered his head in front of mine until I couldn't avoid looking at him any longer. "Fighting with you in the pouring rain. Smoking you on the basketball court. Getting you to play in front of the kids." His mischievous grin gave way to a look of transparency. "Feeling your heart race in my arms."

I staggered backward, afraid he'd misinterpret the sound of my heart racing now. It wasn't what he thought.

He strode forward, not letting me slip away. "Those memories are mine, Em. They'll always be mine."

They were my memories too. The pain of losing them trekked up my throat.

He moved closer still. The doorframe brushed against my back as he raised my chin. "Does it have to be this way?"

No matter how many times I'd asked myself the same question, the answer never changed.

I caged my tears behind my lashes. "Yes."

Silence pressed in. I straightened and grasped for strength to remain steadfast, for both our sakes.

A pained smile creased his face. "You'll always hold a piece of my heart too." He took off his ball cap, ran his fingers through his hair, and tugged it back on. When he looked up again, the smolder in his expression hadn't waned. "So, I won't lie to you this time. I'll respect your decision and say goodbye, but I won't let go of what we had, Em." He shook his head. "Not ever."

Oceans of promise poured from his eyes to mine. I turned to leave before my resolve crumbled. Halfway down the hall, I stopped and curled my fingers around the reminder of why I'd come to begin with. The center needed him.

A deep breath led me around. "I came to give you this." I handed him the photocopy of Dee's transcribed memories. "You need to know the difference you made in Dee's life. The difference you've made in all the kids' lives." I folded my hand over his. "Please don't give that up because of me."

A. J.'s focus drifted down to the note, but he didn't respond. I strode through the door again without stopping to look back.

The path to my apartment stretched longer than it should have. Same as my thoughts. Truth was, I couldn't control A. J.'s reaction any more than I could change Ms. Mendierez's. We each made our own choices. And for now, my only choice was to keep walking.

7

INFERNO

WAITING for a response from A. J. was as hard as waiting for word back on my grant requests. Seeing that "For Rent" sign on Monday hadn't helped matters.

How could Mr. Glyndon boot us out like that? The center had been there for years. Yeah, money had been tight recently, but Trey was trying. We all were. I thought he saw that.

Irritated all over again, I rotated the car vent and tugged my scarf away from my neck. My cell rang from the passenger seat. Without looking away from the road, I groped for my phone. "Hello."

"Miss E?"

"Darius? Is everything okay?"

"Yeah, yeah. I mean, I think so. But Trey... he was on the phone with that landlord guy. I heard somethin' 'bout him reneging on the three-month deal."

What? My inferno setting kicked up ten degrees. I

wrestled my scarf off and tossed it in the back. "Are you sure?" Mr. Glyndon couldn't be that heartless. He wouldn't kick us out with Christmas only two weeks away.

"I don't know. Trey was trying to keep it all hush hush, but he was gettin' hot. I could tell. He dipped outside when he caught me staring."

Leave it to Trey to insulate everyone else from the blow. But he wasn't in this alone. *Deep breath.* "Do me a favor. Don't mention it to any of the kids. Keep everyone cool. Business as usual, okay?" I glanced in the rearview mirror. "Let me take care of this."

"Don't go doing nothing crazy. I never met this Mr. G., but I don't trust him."

A smile poked through. Darius might've been seventeen, but his protective instincts were really adorable sometimes. "Nothing crazy. Promise."

"A'ight. I'm out, then."

I dropped the phone on my lap, checked all my mirrors, and busted a U-turn in the middle of the street. We all had our own definitions of crazy.

BY THE TIME I reached the swanky neighborhood, my mind had sprinted home and back at least twice. I had to figure out why Mr. Glyndon was making all these hasty changes.

I cruised up along a curb in front of a winding

driveway leading to a ridiculously posh multi-story home. Even the guy's mailbox had a suite added on it. I choked back an eye-roll. Glad to see he was hurting for that rent money.

A third attempt at calling him went straight to voice-mail. I tossed my cell in the cup holder and rummaged through my purse for a pad and pen. If he wouldn't take my calls, at least he could read a note. One way or another, I'd get through to him.

I jotted down my appeal and looked up as a redhead snuck through the fence in a wraparound skirt and a bikini top that should've been fired for failing at its job. Where'd she come from, and, seriously, who dressed like that in December?

Folding the page in half, I clambered out of the car. "Hi, excuse me?" I jogged toward her. "Is Mr. Glyndon home?"

A cautious glance met me halfway, flitted behind her to the house, and sailed around the neighbors' yards. "Mitch is out of town."

Figured. "Is anyone home I can speak with?"

"Sorry, he's on vacation."

With his wife, no doubt.

The girl lowered her Hollywood sunglasses from her head onto her face and kept scouring the streets while rubbing her arms, clearly anxious to get to her warm car.

If she had any connection to Mr. Glyndon, maybe she'd leak some information. Playing the naive card couldn't hurt. "Do you live here?"

"No, I was…" She spun the back of a long, dangling earring. "Cleaning his Jacuzzi for him."

While modeling for the swimsuit edition of *Sports Illustrated?* Right.

"Will you be *cleaning his Jacuzzi* when he comes back?"

She straightened her shoulders. "Possibly."

I spun the note in my hands, weighing the chances she'd give it to him.

A door opened across the street. She slinked by me. "Sorry, I need to get going."

I moved to let her pass and spotted a silver BMW idling several car lengths down from Riley's Civic. I squinted. Same tinted windows as the one from the other day. Was someone following me? As soon as I started toward it, the car peeled out again and zipped down a side street before I could catch the license plate number. Perfect.

A backward glance turned into a spin. Miss Jacuzzi Cleaner had vanished, and some middle-aged woman in a leopard-printed jacket and high-heeled boots stood across the street with her empty mailbox open as wide as her stare. For a second, I thought someone had thrown me into an episode of *Desperate Housewives.*

My stomach twisted as the pieces melded together. Mr. Glyndon's sudden urgency to close the center, like someone was breathing down his neck. The indiscreet redhead. The gawking neighbor. Was that what this was about? Some kind of blackmail for catching him cheating on his wife? The implications almost bent me in half.

It had to be Tito. His reach never ended. Even in jail, he'd found a way to taunt the center. Was this retribution for Trey not hiding his little brother there? He'd done all he could for the kid. What did Tito expect? A miracle?

Back at Riley's car, I slid into the driver's seat and started a new note to Mr. Glyndon. I didn't care what kind of dirty laundry he had. He couldn't cower to Tito's threats.

A ring lit up my cell with the same strange number from the other day. I peered around for any sight of that BMW and tentatively swiped the screen. "Hello?"

"Miss Matthews?" a woman with an all-business tone asked.

I checked my mirrors. "Yes."

"Hold, please."

"Wait, what?" Instrumental music came through the line.

Someone picked up a moment later. "Emma, my girl, so glad to get in touch. Nick Copeland, here."

Riley's boss? What in the world?

He didn't even pause for a response. "Listen, I don't want to tie you up. We're all busy, right?" The conversations in the background punctuated his point. "Yeah, Sue, thanks. Tell him I'll be there in five," he said away from the phone.

The buzz of voices dwindled behind what sounded

like a door closing. "So, Emma, I gotta tell ya, the music industry could use more winners like you. With all the drama these days, we don't see a girl supporting her man in his career as much as we used to. It's really something special. Riley's a lucky guy."

Did all businessmen have to be schmoozers? Thankfully, he couldn't see my eyes rolling through the phone. "I'd say you ended up being the lucky one, landing a deal with him. I'm sure his level of talent doesn't come around every day." Two could play this game.

He took a sip of something. "Mm. Don't I know it? All he has to do is hit the first stage, and he'll build a fan base so fast, he'll shoot to stardom overnight."

And make you rich in the process. A businessman through and through.

"But my real luck would be having you on board with Riley's tour schedule."

And there it was. Motives exposed.

I shimmied up in my seat, defenses rising. "Of course I'm on board. I only want the best for him—"

"That's what I'm talking about. A real winner. Knew I could count on you to convince him to stop bucking." He took another swig of his drink. "Collaboration is refreshing, isn't it? So much better than having to get lawyers involved."

Wow. Apparently, I could add underhanded threats to his list of charming traits. Was he going to sue Riley if he breached his contract? Was that what Jess had meant was the best part?

A line beeped in the background. "Listen, honey, business calls. You know how it is with these creative types. It's a nonstop job, talking clients into knowing what's best for their careers."

I looked back at Mr. Glyndon's house and at the way the world worked. *You could always blackmail them.*

8

HOME

STUDYING for finals was the only thing distracting me from thinking about Nick's call. Well, that and recurring trips to Paradox Café. All week, Jaycee and I'd joined the frenzy of students boosting our caffeine intake before cramming for exams. The extra surge had pulled us through late nights and early mornings. Afternoons, however, were another story.

Jaycee lay sacked out on the couch, arm hanging off the side, mouth open, looking exactly how I felt.

I tossed my stats book off my lap and tiptoed across the living room. My phone buzzed from my pocket.

"Hello?" I whispered.

"Is this Miss Emma Matthews?"

I smiled at the sound of Riley's voice and played along. "Yes."

"The same Emma Matthews who's engaged to Riley Preston?"

"The one and only."

"Good. Then I have a very important message for you. He'd like you to know he's dying to see you when his flight comes in today."

"Today?" I clamped my hand over my mouth and spun toward Jaycee. She didn't so much as flinch at my outburst. I slipped around the partition wall into the kitchen. "Why didn't you tell me you were coming in today?"

"Well, I know how you love surprises." A grin slid through his voice. "And getting to hear that *excited* response was well worth the wait."

"Aw, sorry, babe," I backpedaled. "Of course I'm excited. You just caught me off guard. It's been a little crazy here. These late nights are starting to take a toll. You should see me. I'm a hot mess."

I picked at the frayed edges of my sweatshirt until my brain finally caught up to the conversation. *Flight. Today.* How much time did I have to get ready? "When do I need to be at the airport?"

"Oh, I wouldn't worry about that. I made other—"

A knock rippled into the foyer of the apartment.

"Hang on one sec. Someone's at the door." I glanced at Jaycee, but the noise didn't appear to disturb her either. Jeez, the girl slept through anything.

My phone dropped to the floor before the door fully opened. "Riley? How did you...? When did you...?" It didn't matter. Nothing held me back from jumping into the only thing that did.

"Now *that* response was definitely worth waiting for." He loosened his arms but held me with his eyes. "I'm home, Em."

Home. I lifted on my toes to kiss him. *Me too.*

A yawn seeped out from under the pillow covering Jaycee's face.

Without moving a muscle, I slanted a glance toward the couch. Jaycee rolled over and nuzzled into the crease between the cushions, hidden from the afternoon sunlight and any awareness of our presence.

Riley motioned to the stairwell. "Let's take a walk," he whispered.

I hurled another once-over down my sweatshirt, tattered jeans, and Converse sneakers. I probably could've used a shower. Or at the very least, a fresh set of clothes. But like everything else in that moment, aside from being with Riley, my appearance was irrelevant.

I eased the door closed and followed him outside. The wind picked up the farther we walked. I pulled my shirt cuffs over my fingers as we rounded the last bend leading to the sports field.

"Man, I've missed this place." Riley shuffled in a circle over the frozen blades of grass. His reminiscent gaze surveyed our favorite spot on the campus and landed on me. His forehead pinched. "Knowing you were here, making memories I wouldn't be a part of... It was kind of excruciating." He faced the sky. "I still have no clue what I was thinking, going there without you."

"We've already been through this."

"I know, and you're right. I needed to go to Nashville as much as you needed to stay here." He raised his shoulders. "Didn't make it any easier."

I flicked my bangs off my lashes. "Tell me about it."

He caressed his thumb over the back of my hand. "I'd do it all over, though—walk through the pain of being apart, as long as it brought us to where we are now." A grin followed. "But if it's all the same to you, I'd really prefer not to let you go ever again."

I draped his arms around me, one at a time, and looked from my engagement ring back to him. "Guess it's a good thing you'll never have to."

Flashes of Nick's call butted into the moment with the reminder that that wasn't entirely true. As much as I didn't care for the guy or his tactics, I couldn't get around admitting he was right. Riley belonged on tour. We'd have to be apart again, but it would be different this time. I wouldn't let anything come between us.

Riley held my gaze. "Promise?"

"Always."

The slightest hue of doubt tinted his eyes. But as he rested his hand on the small of my back, he tucked away whatever had pulled at his brow a moment before. "Dance with me."

By now, I'd learned to stop asking if he meant dance right where we were, without any music. To him, music never stopped. Which was exactly why he should be out there, sharing that gift and passion with fans. I had to come up with a way to convince him that was the right choice.

I set my chin over my hand on his shoulder, thoughts swaying with our feet.

He rested his cheek against my temple. "You know, I've been thinking. Maybe we don't have to wait until summer to get married. Why not after winter break? We can even go to Vegas if you want."

I tilted back. "But I thought you—"

"I thought I had a lot of things figured out." He curved flyaway strands of hair around my ear. "Jackson's moving out in January. We can live in my apartment here until you finish school. Nashville will still be there when we're ready."

But would his career?

His phone rang. He tipped it out of his pocket and strained to keep a smile in place. He kissed my cheek, swiped the screen, and turned to take the call. "Yeah, Brett, what's up?"

What did his agent want? I rubbed my hands over my arms but couldn't shake the sense Riley was still down-playing this thing with Nick. And where'd eloping come from? He was supposed to be the sensible one.

Riley rolled a rock back and forth with his shoe. "Mm-hmm. Got it... So, we're all good? ...Yeah, sure thing. We'll be in touch... Yep. I appreciate it, man. Later."

His shoulders rose and fell before he turned. "Sorry

about that." He drew me into the same position where we left off.

Like that was happening. I set a hand on his chest and looked him in the eyes. "Riley, I love you for wanting to protect me, but I need to know what's going on."

"Brett's taking care of it."

"Of what?"

Exhaling, he stared at the grass and kneaded his shoulder blade. "Nick's threatening to pull the album."

My arms came undone. I backed up. "He can't." Our phone call... He hadn't given me enough time to persuade Riley to go.

He scratched his jaw and squinted. "Technically, he can. But I doubt he will. He's too invested. And Brett's already found a loophole in the contract anyway."

"A loophole?" That didn't sound sketchy or anything. "Why doesn't that give me the warm fuzzies?"

Riley slid forward. "I haven't finished recording that last song. There's no way anything's moving forward until that's finalized."

"Aren't they sort of in charge of making the rules?"

He swayed his head. "I like to think of them as guidelines."

"Riley, you can't push it back. They need you to go. Your fans need you. The—"

"*You* need me."

I looked toward the border of fir trees before he could see any confirmation of the truth in that statement. Of course I needed him, but not at the expense of his future.

If Nick weren't being so hard-nosed about it, we could've compromised—had Riley finish up the last track now and do some local touring until I graduated in May when we could travel together.

His schmoozy voice hadn't left my mind since he'd called. He obviously wasn't the type to take no for an answer. If that was how the industry worked, fine. Why wouldn't Riley just go along with it?

"Do you even want to tour?"

He paused so long, I was afraid to meet his eyes again. "I want you more."

I gripped the necklace Dad had given me and stared at the empty bleachers. "Please don't put me in the middle. You'll end up—"

"Can we not fight about this right now?" Assurance back in place, he laced his hands around my waist and tugged my torso close to his. "Come home with me for Christmas. We can talk about wedding plans after, okay?"

I exhaled a prayer. *Please help us through this.*

Maybe spending the break with him would give me the time I needed to change his mind, but the prospect of meeting his family sent one reason to worry chasing another. "You haven't been home in years."

He dug the tip of his sneaker in the dirt. "Yeah, but after being back in Nashville—I don't know—I just feel like it's time."

That was for sure. Still, I couldn't imagine anything more awkward than showing up to the family he'd left behind in anger after a blowup with his dad.

"Sorry, I'm trying to picture this." I impersonated him approaching the house. "Hi Mom. Hi Dad. I haven't been home in over four years but thought I'd drop in. I'm about to tour with a major record label. And oh, by the way, this is my fiancée, whom you've never met in your life." I cocked my chin at him.

His amusement gave way to sobriety. "I actually went home once—summer before my senior year. Jasmine was in the hospital. She didn't know I came. No one did except my mom." He scratched the back of his hair. "I wasn't ready…"

"And now you are?"

"Hope so." He released a hard breath and took my hand. "I need you there with me, Em."

Then I couldn't afford to be anywhere else. "Okay."

Riley draped one side of his coat around me while we walked back to the apartment, but the fear of meeting his dad kept slicing through with the wind.

We strolled up beside his Civic. "I think I can handle Jake giving me the cold shoulder for leaving him with Jackson till we get back, but your mom's not going to hate me for stealing you for the holidays, is she?"

"You kidding me? After you invited her to the lake house when you proposed, you can do no wrong."

He brandished the self-conscious smile that was way too attractive for its own good.

"It'll be fine. Mom and Austin already made plans of their own. I have to take my last final on Friday, and then I'm all yours."

"It means a lot to me." He reclined against the fender. "My mom will welcome us with open arms. My dad's another story. And I have no clue what to expect from my little sisters. I've let them down too many times."

"I doubt any of them have stopped loving you." They'd all be ecstatic to see him. I was sure of it. Seeing *me* on the other hand... I twisted my engagement ring back and forth. "Do you think they'll come to the wedding?"

The corner of Riley's lips climbed up his cheek the way it always did when he was reading between the lines. "They're gonna love you."

I slid the pearl along my necklace, not convinced.

He hooked a finger in my belt loop and drew me toward him. "Stop worrying."

I folded my arms. "Right back at you, buddy."

Both of us should've been experts at the whole conquering fear thing by now. But after as many times as we'd tried to convince each other we were braver than we thought, we might've just found the ultimate litmus test.

9

IMPASSE

THE DRIVE from school to Riley's parents' in southern Oregon was shorter than I expected. With one leg still inside the car, I peered over the hood. A single willow tree stood front and center in the middle of a yard outlined by a split rail fence. In the far corner, an old wooden tractor wheel leaned against the house's brick siding in front of a garden. Throw in a tire swing, and the scene could have passed for a painting.

I followed Riley up the driveway to the front porch, where two empty plant hangers bookended a wind chime playing a love song with the breeze. The atmosphere brimmed with a petition to relax. But even the comfort of standing hand-in-hand with Riley couldn't distract me from the door looming in front of us.

As relieved as I was to have a break from school, I

would've taken the end-of-semester pressure over this restlessness any day.

I shifted my weight from leg to leg, one second standing behind Riley, the next by his side.

The porch light zeroed in on his slanted grin. "Don't worry," he said from the corner of his mouth. "The dog's the only one who bites."

"Very funny." I released his hand long enough to transfer the sweat from my palm onto my pant leg. "Why didn't you call ahead of time to let them know we were coming?"

His smile dropped. He picked at a scrape in the trim. "I think I was afraid they'd tell me not to."

It killed me to hear the heaviness in his voice. I squeezed his hand and searched for the right words, but a creak from inside pulsed across the concrete porch to my feet and shot up to my throat.

The door cracked open and revealed a teenager's silhouette. His sister... Melody? She stayed behind the screen, staring.

Waiting might've been suspenseful but standing there in silence was downright torturous. I looked up at Riley in a silent nudge for him to say something—anything.

She removed her earphones. "What are *you* doing here?"

My fingers tightened around Riley's. If his sister's reaction had caught him off guard, he didn't let on. It was probably no less than what he'd expected.

"Nice to see you, too, Melody."

"It's Mel," she said in a tone as dry as her deadpan stare.

"Okay, *Mel*, mind if we come in?"

Without altering her expression, she opened the door and returned her attention to her phone. A clamor rang from down the hall, followed by someone skidding around the corner in a pair of bright purple socks. "Is that…?"

A girl around ten years old stopped at the opposite side of the entryway. Her hazel eyes stretched open wider than her priceless smile. "Riley!"

He knelt to the floor just in time to meet her running hug. Riley spun her in the air. "Man, I've missed you, kiddo." He set her back down and took in the sight of her. "When did you get so grown up?"

"Hmm," Melody grunted from the corner. "Maybe it was during the last four years you haven't bothered to come home."

My insides constricted at the same time Riley's jaw twitched.

His younger sister, on the other hand, seemed immune to it. She tugged on the bottom of his shirt, cupped her hand around her mouth, and lifted on her toes. "Who's your girlfriend?"

Smiling, Riley knelt to the floor again and turned her to face me. "Jasmine, I'd like you to meet Emma. Emma, this is my baby sister, Jasmine."

She craned her head toward his. "I'm not a baby."

He raised his palms in a plea bargain.

She extended a hand toward me. "You can call me Jazz. You know, like the music."

She couldn't have been any cuter. "It's very nice to meet you, Jazz. You can call me Em."

As much time as I'd spent with kids, you'd think I would've grown accustomed to how easily their faces lit up with the simplest of efforts. But the way Jasmine's countenance sparkled over our introductions was enough to capture my heart single-handedly.

She whirled back to her big brother and tucked her head against his ear. "She's pretty." A giggle trailed her intended whisper.

"Girls? What's going on in here?" A woman's voice soared around the corner right before she did. The dust on her scalloped apron matched the white smudges on her forehead, where she'd probably brushed back the strands falling out of her ponytail.

She dropped a country blue dish towel on the floor and pressed one hand against the wall. The other glided to her chest, then over top of her mouth, and finally resumed its spot over her heart.

"Riley?" The voice that had resounded through the kitchen a moment ago now barely reached a whisper. "W... what are you doing here? When did you...?"

Same as when he'd shown up at my door, the reason didn't matter. She rushed the rest of the way and flung her arms around him.

I should've thought to bring tissues. I backed against the wall, not wanting to intrude on their moment.

Mrs. Preston leaned back ever so slightly from a hug she'd obviously been waiting for some time to give and traced the outline of Riley's face with both hands.

"Mom, I'm so sorry—"

"Shh. Never mind that. There's no use fretting over water under the bridge. You're home now. That's what matters."

No question where Riley's compassion and tender-heartedness came from.

Melody stalked down the hallway, practically side-swiping the pair of them as she passed. Riley's gaze followed her to the corner and dropped to the carpet runner.

"Don't worry about her, sweetheart," Mrs. Preston said. "She's mad at everyone these days. I think it's that music she listens to. Puts her in a right awful state of mind." She held Riley's shoulders and searched his face again. "My, what a handsome young man you are."

"Mom," he moaned.

A laugh spilled out before I could stop it. I wasn't used to seeing him in this context.

"Oh." Mrs. Preston turned toward me.

I couldn't blame her for not noticing me any sooner. It was hard to notice much of anything when Riley was in the room. He had a way of unintentionally stealing the spotlight.

"And who's this?"

The single light bulb in the hallway transformed into a heat lamp homed in on my cheeks.

Riley strode to my side. "Mom, I'd like you to meet Emma Matthews, my fiancée."

I held my breath, waiting. *Please don't be mad.*

An indecipherable expression flooded her face. Without hesitation, she engulfed me in a hug like I was one of her daughters. My throat squeezed. The contented smile on Riley's face from behind his mom made it impossible to swallow the emotion.

Definitely should've brought tissues.

Mrs. Preston held on to my hand, took one of Riley's, and looked back and forth between the two of us with watery eyes. "Thank you for coming home."

Blinking her tears away, she ruffled her hands over her apron and spun toward the kitchen. "You're just in time for dinner."

I followed Riley past the foyer toward savory aromas rivaling those from the Olive Garden. A tug on my shirt drew me to a stop beside a long dining room table.

"Em?" Jasmine asked. "Can I be the flower girl?"

I pinched my lips together and met Riley's glance. "I think we'd both be honored."

He winked in agreement and passed through the open doorway into the kitchen.

Jasmine danced over to a china cabinet against the back wall. "You can help me set the table." She counted the number of necessary place settings and lugged out a tower of plates.

As we circled the table, folding napkins and laying

out silverware, I listened to the conversation coming from the kitchen.

"Where's Dad?" Riley asked.

"He's out back in the shed, working on that motorcycle of his. He'll be coming along in a minute." She laughed. "He has an uncanny way of knowing when dinner's ready."

"Some things never change." The edge in Riley's tone seemed harsher than it needed to be.

I jumped at the sound of Mrs. Preston's knife hitting the cutting board. "You're right. Some things never change. But when you stop trying to change them, you might realize they're not that bad." She left one hand over the knife handle and pressed the other flat on the counter. "Please, Riley. Please don't start. You just got here, and I don't want—"

He was at her side before she could finish. "I'm sorry."

The screen door leading to the backyard swung open and shut. Complete silence swept throughout the house.

I turned to Jasmine for some clue as to what was going on. Her white knuckles stretched over the top of the chair with the answer. This was the moment we'd all been dreading.

TRACES

RILEY'S DAD stopped inside the door, shock flickering across his dark blue eyes. Every crease lining the leathery skin on his forehead pulled taut. A forced blink lasted so long, there was no telling how many thoughts passed with the single motion.

He looked straight at Riley, face devoid of emotion. "The prodigal son returns."

Wind stirred up outside and shook the window screen against the glass.

Mr. Preston finished wiping his hands on a faded rag blotched with mechanical grease while striding toward the refrigerator. He snapped off a bottle cap. "And what's the occasion that graces us with your presence?" Glaring at the ceiling, he guzzled a quarter of his soda down without taking a breath.

The tight grip Mrs. Preston had around Riley's forearm matched the one wrenched around my insides.

Veins enlarged on the tops of Riley's hands as he seized the edge of the counter. "I came to apologize. To set things right." His transparency tore at his words. "I left in anger, and it took me a lot longer than it should've to realize some things aren't worth sacrificing." He loosened his grip and moved a tentative step forward.

Mrs. Preston clutched a dish towel with both hands. Though her gaze had momentarily strayed toward her husband, she locked it on her son now.

Riley approached him, shoulders squared but eyes tenderized with humility. "I'm sorry, Dad. I came back because I'd like my family to be a part of my life."

The glass bottle banged onto the countertop so hard, the echo shuddered over Jasmine and me in the dining room.

"Well, isn't that nice. Rose, look, our son's discovered it's a good idea to be a part of our family."

Mrs. Preston closed her eyes. "Jonathan, please."

Ignoring his wife, he splayed his arms to his sides and lowered his head in a half bow. "By all means, son, welcome home."

On his way through the doorway, he jerked short at the sight of me. If I were Jasmine's size, I would've shrunk behind the chair. Not that I needed to. It took less than ten seconds for Mr. Preston's eyes to dismiss my presence altogether before he charged down the hall. A door slammed, and my shoulders almost hit my ears.

Riley tore through the dining room, his mom on his heels.

"Let him cool off." Mrs. Preston caught his hand. "He'll come around."

The look on Riley's face said differently. If that encounter was any indication, he was probably right.

Mrs. Preston motioned behind her. "Riley, why don't you get the drinks? Emma, would you mind helping me finish up the salad?"

How could she be so calm?

Though, to be honest, I would've taken any diversion right about then. I released the innocent chair and followed her warm smile into the kitchen.

Similar to Trey, she seemed to have a way of defusing the tension, no matter how fierce. Her hospitality ushered an unexplained peace over their home.

I clung to it as long as I could. But once we all sat down at the dinner table less than a half hour later, peace felt nowhere in sight. Or maybe it was just me. Everyone else seemed to avoid the obvious.

Riley raised a fork twirled with spaghetti. "Home-made pasta? Mom, you've outdone yourself."

Jasmine slurped a noodle through her lips. "She's taking a cooking class."

"Not exactly," Mrs. Preston said. "I've been watching a cooking show."

"Yeah, like, every day." Jasmine laughed.

Riley's grin peeked from behind his cup. "Wonder if there's a show on frozen dinners."

Teasing me about my go-to meals never ceased to entertain him.

Mr. Preston dragged his fork across his plate. "So, Emma, why don't you tell us about yourself and why you don't mind being apart from your family over the holidays?"

Riley clanked his glass on the table. "Dad."

I set down my own glass and confined my nervous fidgeting to the napkin in my lap. "It's only my mom, my brother, and me. My dad died when I was sixteen." I stared at my placemat. "Austin's on a snowboarding trip with some friends, and Mom's spending the week with my grandparents, so it worked out. I'm planning to make a trip home during the spring instead."

Mrs. Preston hastened to swallow a sip of tea the second I finished speaking. "And what are you studying at Reed, dear?"

Nice conversation changer. I smiled at the intervention and picked through my salad with my fork. "Business."

"She's brilliant," Riley said with enough animation to compensate for my lack of any.

My face had to have turned the same color as the spaghetti sauce, but Riley didn't give me the chance to object. "Don't let her modesty fool you. She breezes through all her coursework, which is impressive enough. Trust me. But it's what she does in the field that's really inspiring."

Jasmine looked at me from above a piece of garlic bread bigger than her hand. "What do you do *in the field?*"

Even if she didn't understand what that meant, her genuine curiosity was enough to drain the heat radiating off my skin. "I work with an organization in inner-city Portland. We offer kids educational help they most likely wouldn't get otherwise."

Jasmine's sweet eyes blinked as she contemplated my response.

Mr. Preston sliced through a meatball. "Sounds like charity."

I straightened in my chair. He didn't have to like me, but he didn't know a thing about the center. "Actually, it's more of an investment. The kids have a lot to offer back to their community. They just need people who are willing to give them a chance."

My initial rise of offense waned. I couldn't mention the kids without it melting my heart. "I'm pretty sure my time there ends up blessing me more than them."

Mr. Preston gnawed on a piece of bread and avoided my eye contact.

The ceiling fan pushed another round of weighted silence over the table until Mrs. Preston cleared her throat. She folded the ends of a towel over the bread bowl. "And what about you, Riley? What have you been spending your time on since you graduated?"

It was an innocent question—a simple conversation starter in any other scenario. She couldn't have known she'd asked the one question Riley feared having to answer.

After gulping down half his water, he lowered the

cup far enough to mumble, "I've been working on my music."

Mrs. Preston leaned forward in a visible strain to decipher what he'd said. Once it must've registered, she froze, along with everyone else at the table.

Except for his dad.

He smeared his bread in the spaghetti sauce and left it standing upright in the middle of the plate. "Thought you gave that up."

"I did... for a while." Riley covered my hand with his. "But I guess, like the kids Emma works with, I just needed someone to have a little faith in me before I saw my potential."

Though sincere, it felt like a jab—a reminder of his dad's deficiency in that area.

Riley looked at me and gave my hand a squeeze.

I returned it, steeling myself before he disclosed the rest of his news. Knowing the bitterness his dad held on to about his own failed career as a musician, I wasn't sure how he'd handle hearing Riley's success at it.

"I actually just got back from Nashville. I've been recording an album with Momentum Records."

Either the fan stopped working or someone vacuumed all the air from the room. Not even a single exhale slipped through.

Mrs. Preston's fork dropped to her plate. She scrambled to blot out the splattered sauce from the tablecloth. "Riley, that's... that's wonderful, honey. Congratulations. We always knew you were a talented musician."

"So, that's why you came home?" Mr. Preston's chair scraped against the floor as he pushed backward. "To prove you did it without me?"

"What? No. I only wanted—"

Mr. Preston rose from the table. He wiped his mouth with his napkin and tossed it over his half-empty plate. "Excuse me. I've lost my appetite."

Riley flew to his feet. "Dang it, Dad. You want to know why I haven't come home? This. This is why. Can't you just, for once, be supportive of me?" He kicked his chair back, raked his hands through his hair, and faced the china cabinet.

The room stood still.

Riley's arms drooped to his sides as he turned around. Each step toward his dad deepened with earnestness. He stopped in front of him with every emotion laid before him. "I'm your son."

A trace of something unspoken softened Mr. Preston's eyes. He averted his gaze toward the floor and swallowed. When he lifted his head, cold detachment had resumed its hold. "I think you gave up that title a long time ago. Or don't you remember that conversation the summer you left?"

I latched on to the seat on either side of my legs. How could he be so callous? Couldn't he see his son's longing for his affection?

A tendon on Riley's neck throbbed. "In case you didn't notice, I'm standing right in front of you." His voice caved to a whisper. "I came back."

I almost ran to his side.

Mr. Preston's gaze flicked to me and back to Riley. "All I see is a boy chasing foolish dreams and dragging some starry-eyed girl along with him."

Riley got up in his face. "You leave her out of this, or I swear I'll—"

"You'll what?" A harsh laugh grated through a humorless smile. Mr. Preston shook his head. "You have no business getting married. You're still just a kid."

"Enough!" Jasmine blasted to her feet. "Stop it. Both of you. Don't you see what you're doing?" An onslaught of tears paraded down her red cheeks. She wheeled around the table and fled to the back door.

Mr. Preston jutted his chin at Riley. "Don't you think you've caused her enough pain?"

"Like father, like son." Riley backed up but kept him locked in a glare. "I'll make it easy on you. We're out of here."

11

GUARDED

RILEY TOOK OFF AFTER JASMINE. I would've been on his heels if Mr. Preston's stare wasn't keeping me frozen halfway out of my seat. As soon as he disappeared down the hall, I skirted around the table and through the kitchen.

Outside, I stumbled onto a deck perched above a long grassy slope leading to a riverbank. Riley had already reached the edge of the water, where he called up to a small tree house hidden inside an old elm's sturdy branches. When Jasmine opened the bottom door, he climbed the ladder toward a conversation they needed to have alone.

No chance I was going back inside without him. I sat on the deck with my legs hanging off the edge instead. Something moved in the corner. A chocolate Labrador, who could've passed for a much older Jake, hobbled toward me. His tired legs apparently moved far slower than his piqued curiosity. I rubbed his head when his journey finally ended in a collapse next to me. Sitting side by side, we both peered across the yard, waiting.

The quaint view from the front of the house had been misleading. The backyard extended at least a hundred feet downhill. A paddleboat rested upside down underneath a gazebo near two bare hammock stands. The peacefulness of it all swept me in immediately.

"You should see it in the summertime."

I flinched at Mrs. Preston's voice.

"It's really lovely that time of year. Everything comes to life then." She sat down and folded her arms over her knees. "I'm sorry for my husband's behavior. There's no excuse." She petted the old dog, and he rested his head on her lap. "He and Riley have trouble seeing eye to eye."

There was an understatement if I'd ever heard one.

Yet now that I'd seen their broken relationship first-hand, my heart ached for restoration even more than before. "What do you think it'll take for them to work it out?"

"I don't know, dear. I don't know."

We both gazed at the river until a splash in the water interrupted the silence. Two seagulls circled around the ripples. Mrs. Preston rose to her feet and swiped off some crumpled leaves from the back of her pants. "Come on. I'll help you with your bags."

"Riley said we were leaving."

"He'll come around." She held out a hand and smiled with the kind of intuition only a mother could have.

We cut through the house to the driveway, hauled the bags from the trunk over our shoulders, and trudged back up the walkway. She'd retired her apron but still looked every bit as hardworking. Her eyes held a mixture of compassion and bravery. I had to smile. "Riley's a lot like you."

"Like his father, too, I'm afraid—stubborn as a mule."

We both laughed. Too bad we couldn't have stayed on the porch, away from the electricity still brooding inside.

Mrs. Preston looked at me with the same intensity I'd grown accustomed to seeing from Riley. "He loves him, Emma. I know it's hard to see that right now, but Jonathan loves his son. Always has."

I lowered the duffle bag to the ground. "I know. And Riley loves him."

We just had to find a way to make them remember.

Mrs. Preston led the way into the house and down the narrow hallway. She snapped on the light. "You can have Riley's old room. He can sleep on the couch."

We maneuvered through stacks of clutter. "It's become a bit of a storage closet these days," she said, "but you'll at least have a bed. It's only a twin."

I reached for her arm. "It's perfect."

She nodded, laid my bag on the bed, and crossed the room again.

"Mrs. Preston?" I called before she left. "Thanks... for letting us stay."

She smiled as if there'd never been a question.

Exhaustion closed in after only two seconds of

sitting down. I hopped right back up. Any longer on the mattress, and I wouldn't have been able to stay awake to wait for Riley. I ambled around the room toward a desk topped with an array of picture frames from his childhood. I lifted one up and laughed. The guitar he held was at least twice his size.

"Every guy's worst fear," he said from the doorway. "Bringing his fiancée home to see all his embarrassing baby pictures."

"Luckily for you, your fiancée has much worse baby pictures. Trust me." I returned the frame. "Though, I was expecting to find a few cute little league pictures mixed in here somewhere."

He caressed the tops of my shoulders from behind. "When you grow up in a family of musicians, ambition to play sports kind of falls by the wayside."

I turned to face him. His eyes had released all traces of his earlier anger.

"I'm sorry you had to see that. My dad doesn't exactly bring out the best in me." He shook his head. "I don't know why I thought it'd be different."

"Because." I curled the sides of his henley in my fingers. "It's your natural default to hope for the best."

"You sound like my mom."

"You must be rubbing off on me then. You're more like her than you realize."

"I'll take that as a compliment."

"Good," I answered. "It was intended to be."

He edged in. "Does that mean you still want to marry me?"

It wasn't fair that his smile still made my heart race.

"Now that you mention it," I teased. "I might need a little more convincing."

"Really?" He kissed the corner of my mouth. "And what kind of convincing did you have in mind?" His lips hovered behind my ear.

I clasped his sleeve. "I'm pretty sure it's going to involve a lot more of that."

"More of what?" His lips glided down my neck until I laughed at how much it tickled.

When his eyes found mine again, he held my gaze with complete sincerity. "I'm glad you're here with me, Em."

"Me too." A sliver of the moon reflecting off the water through the window caught my eye. "Why didn't you tell me you lived on such a beautiful property?"

He shrugged. "It belongs to my grandparents." He walked over to the window and rested his forearms on the sill. "After we got kicked out of that dingy apartment in Nashville, we had nowhere to go. Gramps said they were ready to move into a condo. That this place had gotten too much to keep up with." He scratched his cheek, laughing sadly. "More like he was trying to clean up his son's mistakes."

No wonder Riley was so cautious about his career in the music industry—so scared of repeating his father's mistakes, terrified of putting that pursuit above his commitment to me. Nick couldn't possibly understand the history that played into Riley's decisions. If he had, he wouldn't have been counting on me to change his mind. What could I say to convince Riley his experience would turn out differently? That it was worth the risk?

"You're not the same person."

He didn't move. "You honestly believe that after today?"

How could he ask that? "Of course I do." I swallowed. "Which is why going on tour is the right decision."

He turned. "Why are you fighting me on this?"

"I'm not. It's just…"

"What?"

Head down, I rubbed the top of my sock with my other foot. "Nick called me last week. Basically threatened things would turn legal if I didn't persuade you to uphold the contract."

I risked a glance up from the oak floor. Riley's nostrils flared.

I hurried over. "I'm sorry. I only want what's best for you."

His chest rose and fell with a lengthy breath. "I know." He kissed the crown of my head. "You're what's best for me, Em. Please trust me in that." He diverted his focus to the bed. "It's been a long day. You should get some sleep."

"You're good with not leaving?"

He tugged on his ear. "Nick isn't the only one who

can be convincing." A soft laugh petered into an exhale as he hung his head. "I owe it to Jazz to stay."

Being here, feeling his heartache as my own, made the reason he'd left me last year seem so clear now it hurt. I closed him in my arms, wanting to take it all away and restore what he'd lost with his family.

He rolled back the covers. Unwillingly, I traded the comfort of his warmth for the blankets'. He leaned down to kiss my forehead and let his lips linger over my skin longer than usual. "Good night, Emma."

"Good night."

Once the door closed behind him, my eyelids had no problem shutting out the day. Unlike my thoughts, which weren't so accommodating.

I wasn't sure how his contract would affect our wedding date. But now that I'd met his family, I couldn't imagine getting married without them there. They *needed* to be a part of it, a part of our lives. All of them.

I rolled onto my side, then onto my back, and stared at the ceiling. *Sleep. You can do it.*

Useless. I fumbled over the handful of items on the nightstand in search of my cell. The lighted screen cast a glow over the wall behind me as it rang.

"I was starting to wonder if you were going to call," Austin said, skipping hellos.

"The phone does work both ways."

"Funny, yours only seems to work in the middle of the night."

I glanced at the clock. It wasn't even midnight yet.

And he called *me* dramatic. "Funny," I said right back, "you're always up when I call."

His laugh echoed through the line. "Someone has to stay up to show these fools how to snowboard."

"You're snowboarding now? In the dark?" His girlfriend wasn't giving him flak for that?

"If we only boarded in the day, it wouldn't be called an extreme sport, now would it?"

I bunched the covers under my arms. "You better be careful."

"You know me."

That was the problem.

"So, you gonna tell me what's up, or not?"

I ran my fingers along the stitching across the comforter. "I can't sleep."

"Your trip to the almost-in-laws isn't turning into a *Meet the Fockers* scene, is it?"

I squeezed my pillow. He was lucky he wasn't here to get a good smack with it. "I'm trying to be serious."

His laughter tapered. "Sorry. Switching over to Emma-mode now. Okay, go."

If I wasn't so distracted, I might've been able to think of a comeback. I sighed into the phone instead. "Riley and his dad don't get along. I mean, I knew that before coming, but it's kind of painful to watch." More than I'd expected.

I stared at his childhood pictures cloaked in moonlight. "We're lucky. We got to share more love in the years we had with Dad than some people do in an entire lifetime. I'm scared they won't see what they're forfeiting until it's too late."

"If Riley upholds the character I've seen in him so far, he won't let that happen."

I wanted so much for Austin to be right, but the scene from dinner replayed in the shadows with the reminder that it was a two-man show.

Background conversations seeped in from his end of the line. He needed to get back to his friends, but there was one more thing on my mind.

"Austin," I said slowly, "there's something I've been meaning to ask you." I rolled the top of the comforter down to my knees and let it unfurl. This was harder than I thought. "Since Dad can't be here, would you walk me down the aisle... on my wedding day?"

I sank deeper into my pillows the longer his pause stretched.

"I wouldn't have it any other way," he said.

The beginning of tears coated my throat. No matter what else changed, I'd always need my brother. "Aust..." My voice cracked.

"Love you, too, Em. Now, get some sleep."

"Night."

The glimmer of light from my phone faded. In a house of fractured memories, I closed my eyes and tried to drift into a dream where everything in life was whole.

THE SPLINTER in Riley and his dad's relationship widened the longer we were there, even on Christmas Eve.

While Mr. Preston tinkered out in the garage, the rest of us hung out in the family room around an artificial tree decorated in mismatched ornaments. I rocked in a recliner, listening to Jasmine show off her saxophone skills. Melody kept her nose buried in a book and her headphones on, as usual. And Mrs. Preston wielded a cross-stitch needle while Riley filled her in on his upcoming album.

His cell vibrated on the end table. One glance at the screen, and he ignored the call. Same as he'd done five times over the last few days. It was probably Jess, or maybe Nick, hounding him about his contract. He couldn't keep ignoring them.

I checked my own cell for any notifications. No new updates since Trey had called yesterday to let me know he'd gotten rejection notices on some of my grant requests, but he managed to talk our landlord back into the original notice he'd promised us. With how easily Mr. Glyndon seemed to be swayed, I wasn't inclined to hold my breath. And right now, Riley's situation was all my heart could handle focusing on, anyway.

Mrs. Preston rubbed her bare feet on the dog. "And when will you go on tour, dear?"

It took all my willpower not to shout, "See, even your mom knows you should be on tour!" I drew my legs into the chair with me and tucked my ankles under them, straining to keep the words from spilling out.

A peanut soared across the room and nailed me in the cheek. Riley's mischievous grin glowed from the launching pad. Apparently, he'd interpreted my expression. No words necessary.

My cell vibrated as I dodged another incoming missile.

"Hello?" I covered my free ear with my hand to block out the music and conversations carrying on in the Preston's family room. "Mom, wait. Slow down. I can't understand you."

I ducked into the hallway, away from the noise. "Okay, sorry. What were you saying?"

A tear-streaked breath shook her pause.

"Mom?"

"Emma, honey." Another shaky inhale. "Austin's been in an accident."

12

PERSPECTIVE

I CLENCHED the top of my hair. "Riley, you gotta drive faster." With San Francisco being at least nine hours from his parents' place, we had to make up time somehow.

"I don't think getting a speeding ticket is going to help." He steadied my antsy knee. "I'm going to get you there. Try to relax."

"Relax?" *Seriously?* I dug my nails into the center console.

Why hadn't Austin listened to me when I told him to be careful? We knew plenty of people who'd been injured in skiing accidents. Broken tailbones, arms, legs. One of our friends from high school even ended up paralyzed from the waist down. I boxed out the image of Austin in a wheelchair. "I can't believe that's all my mom told me."

"I'm sure she told you everything she knew."

Leave it to Riley to be patient and levelheaded.

I coiled the seat belt around my finger. "I know. But if anything were to happen to him…" I couldn't even go there. I squeezed my eyes shut. *God, please let him be okay.*

"Em, look at me." Riley pried my hand from the seat belt and wove his fingers through mine. "Everything's going to be okay. Why don't you try to get some sleep?"

Sleep? Wow, levelheaded and insane. How did that work?

A grin snuck up his cheeks, as if he'd heard my thoughts.

"By the time we get to see him, you're going to wish you would've slept while you had the chance."

He was right. Of course. I buried my pillow under my arms, along with the comment I wanted to make, and focused on the pine trees passing along the highway. Sunbeams streaked through the branches and sprawled over my face.

"Here." Riley shimmied off his sunglasses and passed them to me. "The sun won't be down for another hour. These'll help." He lowered his visor, kissed my hand, and set it in his lap.

Patient, levelheaded, and sacrificial.

He squinted down the endless highway ahead of us, and I stared at every reminder of why I was marrying him, until that single comfort lulled me to sleep.

RILEY'S THUMB smoothed over the back of my hand. The clock blinked into focus. 2:00 a.m. Between fits of in-and-out sleep, I'd changed a dozen positions, but he hadn't let go. "We're almost there," he said.

I checked my cell. No missed calls, just a text from a number I didn't recognize: *At UCSF's Medical Center.*

The light pollution coming from downtown San Francisco led us the rest of the way. As soon as the wheels breached the parking spot, I unbuckled my seat belt, felt for the automatic unlock lever, and dashed outside.

The hospital's entrance opened down the middle and released an antiseptic-scented breeze from inside. I latched on to Riley's arm as we approached the receptionist.

"I'm here to see my brother."

A pepper-haired woman lifted a glance from her desk. Beside her, a red light lit up on a phone with at least twenty lines. She started to reach for it.

I stretched over the counter to stop her. "It's urgent."

The woman could've fit two of me in between her broad shoulders. Her glare alone nearly squeezed me in half. I prudently removed my arm from the ledge. She returned her attention to her computer screen. "Your brother's name?"

"Austin. Austin Matthews."

She drilled her nails over the keyboard. Each stroke jacked up my blood pressure until it hammered in my ears. The lights on her phone lit up again. She balanced the receiver between her ear and shoulder and continued typing. "UCSF's Medical Center, how may I direct your call?"

Riley rested a calming hand against my back as I craned my neck to the ceiling.

Someone staggered toward us from the waiting area.

"Anna? What are you doing here?" My brother's old college friend was the last person I'd expected to see.

She stretched with a yawn. "Your mom called me a few hours ago. Asked if I'd wait out here for you."

I couldn't help staring at her. Austin and Anna used to be close. But ever since he started dating Hailey, Anna had basically become a nostalgic memory.

"I don't know why," she said.

A woman toting a little boy on her hip flitted past us, pulling my gaze after them.

"You don't know why, what?" I said almost absently.

"Why your mom called me instead of someone else. That's what you were thinking, right?"

"How did you know...?"

Anna smiled. "You're a lot like your brother. Your eyes speak your thoughts louder than most words."

I stared at the tiles before my hot cheeks added any more thoughts to the conversation. "Sorry. It's just that I know you and Austin have sort of lost touch."

"I'm guessing my number was the first one your mom could find."

If Mom was in that much of a rush, how bad did that make things?

The receptionist coughed away from the phone, drawing my attention again. "Yes, ma'am. Hold please." She transferred the call, hung up, and made a few more clicks with her mouse. "Austin Matthews. He's in room 234."

That was all I needed. I launched off the counter and flew up the stairs. On the other side of some double doors, I almost knocked over a pair of nurses coming in the opposite direction. Riley and Anna apologized on my behalf on their way through.

The white sterile walls turned the long hallway into a perfect acoustic sound system for all the beeping monitors. Squares of speckled tiles blurred past my feet until I saw Mom standing in front of a window to one of the rooms.

"Mom, I got here as fast as I could."

She held me tight. "I'm sorry I couldn't call. The reception in here stinks."

"Is he...?"

"He's going to be fine, honey." I followed her nod to the window. The last of the adrenaline holding me together tanked at the mere sight of my brother with monitors and tubes connected to his strong, infallible body.

She motioned to the room, and Riley tipped his head in a nudge.

I pushed the heavy door open wide enough to slip through without letting too much of the outside noise in. Austin's heartbeats pulsed on the echogram. I treaded lightly and withered into the chair beside his bed. Between the strain from being at the Preston's, the fatigue of being overtired, and the angst of worrying if Austin was okay, I almost lost it.

"Still overly dramatic." A half-dazed grin paraded across his face.

I leaned against the side of the mattress.

His focus flitted from his left leg propped up in a cast back to me. "How would you feel about being rolled down the aisle?"

I shook my head at him. "How about you just concentrate on healing, okay?"

His laugh turned into a wheeze, as if it hurt to move. "You worry like Mom."

"And you don't worry enough." I sat back, arms crossed. "What were you thinking?"

"It's not like I instructed that sheet of ice to position itself in the middle of my ski jump."

"Well, you should do things that are less dangerous."

He laughed again, this time bracing the movement with his arm. "Now, where would the fun be in that?"

"Seriously, Aust. If something had happened to you…" I couldn't lose him after losing Dad. He wasn't only family. He was one of my best friends.

"I'm fine." Wincing, he scooted his upper body a little higher on the pillows behind his back. "Come here."

I curled up against his side the way we used to do as kids and tried not to put too much weight on him. He rested his head against the top of mine. "Merry Christmas, Emma."

I shot a glance at the clock, the time finally registering. Somewhere in the chaos, the night had stretched into the wee hours of Christmas morning.

"Merry Christmas," I whispered back.

It didn't take long for Austin's breathing to deepen into an unconscious rhythm. I scooted off the bed as gingerly as possible and peered out the window toward the other person in my life who meant the world to me.

Before the door had fully shut behind me, Riley had me enclosed in his arms.

I set my chin on his chest and looked up into his fiercely compassionate eyes. "I'm sorry. I've been so—"

"No apologies necessary."

The exhaustion on his face pummeled a wave of guilt through me, nonetheless. He hadn't even had a chance to rest yet.

Anna's sneakers squeaked over the floor as she reached for the door handle. "May I?"

"Of course." I stepped out of the way.

Inside, she moved the chair a little closer to the bed and sat on the very edge of the cushion with her elbows pressed against the mattress. She looked over Austin, surveying the condition of his tethered body, and gently slipped her hand under his.

No wonder Mom had thought to call her. That reminded me. "Mom?" I spun to face her. "Where's Hailey? Wasn't she on the trip with Austin?"

"According to Mike, she's still there on the mountain."

I blinked. Twice. How could his girlfriend not have come with him to the hospital?

Mom shrugged. "Guess they still had a couple more days left on the timeshare."

Was that supposed to be a suitable answer? Not that it mattered. No explanation would've reversed the permanent damage to my estimation of Hailey's commitment to my brother.

Mom didn't bother pressing the issue. She set her cold hands over Riley's and my forearm. "Why don't you two go home? Get some sleep." She looked back through the window. "I think Austin's well taken care of for the evening."

Riley almost tripped over his feet as he turned. I caught his elbow. "I'll drive."

BACK HOME, Riley trailed me down the hall. The empty house amplified each creak in the oak floorboards. I flicked on the light switch. Unlike Riley's old room-turned-storage-locker, mine looked pretty barren with most of my things away at school.

That sassy smile of his crawled up his cheek. "No baby pictures?"

"You must've missed the hallway walls."

I beat him to the doorway and stretched my arms across the jamb.

"Can't keep me locked in here forever."

"I can try." I backed him away from the door.

He followed my eyes to the twin bed lining the far wall and shook his head. "Not happening."

I crisscrossed my arms. "Don't try to tell me you're not exhausted. You need to sleep."

"Yeah, on the couch," he insisted.

"Fine. But stay with me for a little while. Please?"

His eyes spoke his usual response before any words. "Just until you fall asleep."

His expression softened the moment he lay beside me.

I snuggled into his warmth, nestled my head under the overgrown stubble on his cheek, and soaked in his faded Nautica scent. "Thanks," I whispered. "For getting me home safely, for being here with me."

He settled a hand over mine on his chest. "Guess we both needed each other this break."

I smiled against his thermal shirt.

As his breathing slowed, the cares of the last week gradually drained until the only thing left was the sweet reminder of how grateful I was for the grace that came with love.

With extra caution, I rolled toward the outside edge of the mattress and eased off as soundlessly as possible. He would be upset with me in the morning for coercing him into sleeping in my bed instead of on the couch, but there really wasn't another option. Whether he wanted to admit it or not, he deserved a good night's sleep.

I paused in front of the kitchen and waited for any signs of stirring from the bedroom. Nothing. All that practice maneuvering down the creaky hallway without waking Mom must've paid off. I crossed the linoleum into Dad's study, where he smiled at me from the Polaroid on his desk.

I didn't need a bed or even a couch when blanketed in the closest thing to his embrace. I stretched out on the carpet under the skylight, watched the stars the way we used to do together, and listened to the memory of the song he'd played for me since I was a little girl. That song would be enough to guide my life no matter where it led next, wouldn't it? I shut my eyes. *Please be enough.*

13

TOUSLED

AFTER A FEW DAYS of random naps on uncomfortable pieces of hospital furniture, we finally got to spend some time at home with Mom and Austin.

I straddled the doorway between the kitchen and living room. "Are you sure you're going to be able to handle things, Mom? This is, like, ten times worse than a man-cold," I called down the hall while eyeing Austin on the couch.

He slid a throw pillow out from behind his back and tossed it at me. "Have you heard me whine once?"

I sat on the sliver of cushion left open beside him and stacked the pillow onto the one already propping up his calf. He tried to pass off a moan for a cough. Nice try. "Mm-hmm. Just don't go getting all soft on me. I don't want to hear about you asking Mom to set a bell next to your nightstand or anything."

He rolled his eyes. "I do have crutches, you know."

Along with a broken leg and fractured ribs.

I looked him up and down. Thankfully, his injuries hadn't been worse. "By the way, just so we're clear. You better never do that to me again. Ever."

He returned my grin from a minute ago.

I threatened to jostle his rib cage. "Promise me, Aust."

"Okay, okay." He held my hands down by my wrists. "As long as you promise I still get to walk you down the aisle." He pointed at his cast. "*Walk* being the operative word, here."

Honestly, I would've let him roll me down in a wheelchair if he had to, but I knew he'd want to stand by my side as Dad would've. "I promise." The ache of knowing Dad would miss both our wedding days pressed in again. That reminded me. "What's up with Hailey staying on the mountain instead of going to the hospital with you?"

Austin picked at the frayed stitching on the twenty-year-old couch. "Guess you'll have to ask her."

I wanted to ask her a few things, all right. "Maybe we should send Anna in instead. I bet she'd show her a few ice patches on the slopes."

The slightest tinge of pink dusted his cheeks. "Friends, Em. Anna and I are friends."

"Mm-hmm."

He shoved me off the cushion.

On my way up, I bumped into my backpack on the floor. The tip of the folder with Dee's drawings in it poked through the opening. With all that had been going on, I'd completely forgotten about them. "Hey, I meant to ask you. Do you think you can help me get some of this artwork printed and see if we can sell any?" I handed him the copies I'd made of Dee's sketches.

"You have a hidden talent you forgot to mention to me?"

His snowboarding accident obviously hadn't knocked the sarcasm out of him.

"They're Dee's—the kid I told you about from the center. It's something I need to do for him, and I was hoping between your connections at work and USC, you might know someone I could work with on it."

He thumbed through the pages. "This is really important to you?"

More than I fully understood. I sat beside him again and toyed with my hoodie's drawstrings. "Guess it doesn't really make sense, but I feel like Dee's art is tied to the center somehow. Like an extension of it. And getting it out there is a way to keep the center going." I dropped the strings. "That sounds stupid, doesn't it?"

Sometimes Austin's smile matched Dad's so much I would've sworn it was his instead. "I'll make a few calls," he said. "We'll see it through."

"Thanks." I hugged him delicately and sat back. "You wouldn't happen to know any gracious benefactors, too, would you?"

"Still no luck on getting a grant?"

I let out a sigh. "One person. If we found just *one* key person to rally behind us, we'd be set." I rose and straightened out my jeans. "Why is that so hard?"

Austin shrugged. "Maybe the timing's off."

"Yeah, well, time better hurry up and get itself together because it's about to run out."

Riley's cell phone rang from across the room. His silhouette faded from the doorway into the kitchen as he took the call.

I shook a finger at Austin. "Stay put for a sec, will ya?"

"Very funny."

Laughing, I skidded into the kitchen. Riley had his back toward me, looking out the sliding door leading to the deck. He held his cell to his ear with the arm he had propped against the trim.

Even from this distance, I could hear Jasmine's level of enthusiasm leaving Riley's in the dust. I ducked under his arm and tried to steal the phone.

"Hang on, Jazz," he said. "Someone here wants to talk to you."

She must've squeaked in a breath during the five seconds it took for Riley to transfer the phone from his ear to mine. As soon as I said hello, a steady stream of ten-year-old musings gushed out. I caught the words "wedding" and "flower girl" before Mr. Preston huffed something in the background.

"Stop it, Dad," she yelled away from the receiver. "They have every right to get married… No, I'm talking to them…"

Mr. Preston got on the line. The same unease we'd experienced at their house slithered across my neck and shoulders again. It took Riley one blink to assess the look on my face and take the phone back.

I didn't hear what his dad said to him. I didn't have to. A hardened shell crept over Riley's countenance and stretched into his voice. "It's not up to you."

He hung up and jammed the phone into his pocket. A moment passed with nothing more than our breathing. He touched his lips to my forehead and left the room without saying anything at all. The front door opened and closed. Even though we were all set to leave, Riley obviously needed another minute without my following him.

Back in the living room, Austin met my anxious eyes but didn't comment.

Mom ambled down the hallway and stopped long enough to notice Riley had gone outside. "Is it that time already?" She hurried into the kitchen and came back with a mini cooler in one hand and two water bottles in the other. "I'll meet you out front, sweetie." She kissed my cheek on her way through the door.

I threw on a beanie, swiped my backpack from the floor, and shuffled over to Austin.

Saying goodbye never got easier.

He inched up into a sitting position while trying not to move his leg. The second I sat down, he squished me into a hug. "Love ya, Em. Stay out of trouble."

"Look who's talking." I leaned back and slid him one more smile. "See ya later... *Softie*." I leaped from the cushion before he could swat me with his pillow again.

"You wait 'til I'm back on my feet," he said as I scurried out the door.

Riley stood at the car, Mom by his side, and sorted through his keys. "Ready?"

Sort of.

Mom bundled me in a hug. "Take care of yourself."

"I will. Love you."

"I love you, too, sweetheart." She held on to my shoulders and looked at me with all the poise and confidence the moment allowed. "You have a wonderful semester, okay? Don't lose sight of that beautiful, strong, loving, young woman I know you are." She traced my necklace, lifted both her hands to my cheeks, and smiled.

In the car, I waved goodbye as we backed out of the driveway. She stayed on the stoop, rubbing her arms. I didn't look away from the side mirror until her reflection trailed out of sight.

"You know," I said. "I could kill Austin for making me worry like that, but I'm sorta glad it worked out for us to spend a few days here."

"Me too."

After that phone call with Mr. Preston, Riley probably wished we had come straight to my house to begin with.

I angled toward him. Whether he wanted to admit it, it hurt him to be at odds with his dad. I saw it on his face. Did he hold any hope of things changing? I twisted my hoodie's drawstrings in a spiral again and tried to unwind my voice. "It'd be nice if your dad could be a part of the wedding."

Riley's foot slipped off the gas pedal. "Are you serious?"

"I was thinking..."

He wrenched the gearshift into third. "Don't waste your time."

His words slammed into me.

He reached across the seat for my hand when I hugged my arms over my torso. "I'm sorry. I just don't want to see you be disappointed."

"Maybe I don't want to see you disappointed either. You're dad's still here..." Without finishing, I stared at the pavement streaming by. It wasn't a guilt trip. I only wanted him to understand what he'd be forfeiting.

A solid minute lapsed before he moved. He lifted the backs of my fingers to his lips. In classic Riley-style, he would let what I said digest before responding.

The first of countless exit signs passed above the car. With the long drive ahead of us, he'd have plenty of time to his thoughts. Trapped in my own, I hunched into the door panel. Maybe there were too many things unsettled for us even to be thinking about wedding plans. I'd been the one lobbying not to put it off, but now I was scared we were rushing.

Glimpses of the skyline sifted through the treetops along the highway. *Please show me what to do.*

SOMETHING BRUSHED AGAINST MY ARM. I peeled my cheek off my seat belt and rubbed out the indent lining my jawbone. My lashes agreed to stay open on the third try when my apartment building fluttered into view. I'd slept the whole way?

I darted up in my seat. My beanie sloped over my forehead and fell onto my lap, dragging sections of hair across my face with enough static electricity to power the car. Nice. Too bad the curtain of stringy hair couldn't have blocked my view of Riley's grin.

At least I didn't leave a puddle of drool on my shirt or something. Did I? Glancing down to check, I laughed. "Nothing like seeing your fiancée when she first wakes up to make sure you know full well what you're getting into."

If the entire trip hadn't already counted as some sort of premarital counseling session, these kinds of unguarded moments had to have gained us some bonus points.

Riley's laugh followed mine. "If that tousled look is supposed to scare me away, then we might have a problem."

I tugged my beanie back on. Not that it helped tame the static electricity or Riley's amusement. I unbuckled my seat belt and resituated my twisted sweatshirt. Thankfully, a shower was only a few steps away.

He yawned. Poor thing. He had to be exhausted.

"I'm sorry you had to drive the whole way."

"You needed to rest. I'm not the one who has a new semester ahead of her."

I reached into the back seat for my bag. "Ugh. Don't remind me." School was the last thing I wanted to think about. "If I have to prep for a new term, then you have to go get some sleep." Probably days of it.

Riley angled his head and squinted. "Deal."

Sometimes that smile made everything else in life feel miles away.

His expression sobered as he glided a thumb over my cheek and wove his fingers into my hair, his eyes rendering words unnecessary.

I rested my hand over his. "I love you too." Above anything else, that one certainty would never waver.

"Em, about the center. Things are gonna work out."

Where'd that come from?

He moved his hand to the headrest behind me. "There are people out there who believe in what you're doing. It's just a matter of finding them."

And not losing faith in the process.

"It'd sure be a lot easier if we didn't have someone sabotaging our efforts."

"What are you talking about?"

I'd been so caught up with everything, I hadn't even told him about my theory yet. "I think Tito has someone on the outside blackmailing our landlord. I went by his place and caught some mistress there. And this silver BMW keeps cropping up, like someone's tailing us."

Riley wriggled up in the seat. "Wait, wait. What? Someone's following you?"

Now I remembered why I hadn't said anything. Same reason I hadn't mentioned it to Trey. "It's probably a scout, poking around and reporting info back to Tito. I've never seen him leave the car."

"Have you called the cops?"

"I'm sure they'd be highly interested in my conspiracy theory and lack of evidence."

He didn't laugh. "If anyone comes near you..."

"I think it's about the center, not me."

"Like last time?"

He had me there. But this felt different, even if I couldn't explain it. "I'm not saying it couldn't be dangerous, but what are we supposed to do? I'm not gonna cower to threats. Tito's not winning this one. I don't care how far he thinks his power flexes."

Riley blew out a breath. "Just promise me you won't go near the center alone."

"I promise. Trey's always there." I rummaged through my purse for the pepper spray. "And I have backup, just in case." I brandished the can and my best disarming smile.

Riley's taut muscles gradually relaxed. Being overtired wasn't helping matters.

"Listen, you can drive me into work each day, okay? But right now, you need to get some sleep." I stretched over the console to kiss his cheek. "Love you."

I climbed out of the car into January's frosty air,

turned to offer one more nod, and trudged up the walk-way. Riley didn't leave until I unlocked my door.

Inside my apartment, I tossed my hat and bag on the couch.

"Hey." Jaycee flittered into the room with a giant mug of something chocolatey snuggled between her hands. A quick once-over ended in a laugh. She flagged me into the kitchen. "C'mon, I'll make you a cup. You look like you could use it."

"That bad, huh?"

She pointed at my reflection in the microwave door. It was worse than I thought. Nothing short of an entire conditioner bottle would rescue me. Well, that, and maybe hot chocolate. The teakettle's whistle convinced me to put off my shower a little longer.

I plopped down beside Jaycee at the kitchen table and blew into my mug. "Nice highlights, by the way."

"Thanks." She fluffed out her hair. "A little new-semester spruce."

As if she ever needed an excuse to see her hairdresser.

"How was your break?"

I lowered my mug to the table. "Eventful."

She raised a brow.

"I'll fill you in later. What about you? I'm surprised to see you back this soon."

"Yeah, I know. It was great to be home, but I felt like I needed to come back early, get my bearings." She pushed away from the table and strode over to the kitchen counter. Whatever she wasn't saying pulled at her shoulders.

"How's your mom doing?" *Please don't be bad news.*

Jaycee set her mug down and leaned both hands on the counter. "We got the test results back from her last appointment."

My muscles tightened. All the possibilities of what could've been causing her mom's health problems tore through my mind in one merciless push.

"She has Lupus." Jaycee secured her mug in both hands again and inched around. "The doc put her on a strict diet. Said that and treatment should simulate a pretty normal life for her."

My pent-up breath tumbled out.

Jaycee's gaze bounced away from mine and rebounded off every square inch of the kitchen. "All the stuff going on with my mom got me thinking over the break." Without finishing her thought, she pivoted to face the counter again. A second later, she spun back around and clamped her lips together like she was battling some inner war over whether to say whatever she was thinking. "Trev and I decided to move up the wedding to March. Spring break, actually."

Once she'd finally blurted it out, she rushed over to the table and cupped my hand. "Listen, I know you and Riley have been thinking of getting married sooner too. We can try to plan both at the same time, but I didn't want to interfere with—"

"Jae, I'd push mine back in a heartbeat for you." I

waved off her unwarranted concern. "Seriously, don't give it another thought." At the rate things were going, we'd have to hold off on ours, anyway, and planning Jaycee's perfect day was much more important to her than mine was to me.

She practically drilled a hole into the table with her stare. "There's one more thing."

I dipped my head under hers, waiting.

"Trev made me promise to talk to you about it first. So, just hear me out."

This couldn't be good. "Okay, you're kinda starting to freak me out now."

She forced a smile and tossed her hands in the air. "It's not a big deal."

"Really? 'Cause that nervous twitch you've got going on says otherwise."

She snagged her half-emptied mug off the table and locked her fingers through the handle. The antsy energy channeled from her hands to her feet and propelled her into a back-and-forth pace across the kitchen floor.

"Trev and A. J. have become close friends over the last couple of years."

"Ye-ah?" I dragged out the word.

"So, when it came time to start thinking about who to have in the wedding party, Trev really wanted A. J. to be the best man."

"That's what you're all worked up about?" I hunched into the back of my chair. "Jae, it's fine. Whatever happened between A. J. and me has nothing to do with your wedding." I tossed a balled-up napkin at her. "Good grief, girl. You were starting to give me heart palpitations for a second there."

Her straight-faced expression cut off my laugh.

She downed the rest of her hot chocolate. "Since you're the maid of honor, you'll, um, have to walk down the aisle with him."

I met her on the floor to intercept her pacing. "I don't know why you're making such a big deal out of this. I think I can handle walking beside A. J. for thirty seconds."

Her face scrunched. "There's more. I've always wanted the wedding party to dance at the reception. So..."

My hamstrings found the edge of my chair.

"It's only one dance... and a few rehearsals." She bit her lip.

One dance. With A. J. In front of Riley. The implications trapped my response somewhere behind my ribs.

"I can tell Trev to ask someone else—"

"It's fine, Jae. I'm sure it'll be fine." We were all adults, right? We could put aside everything else for a single day. This was our friends' wedding we were talking about here. It'd work out... as long as I made it through telling Riley first.

14

ENOUGH

"No way." Riley's shoes gripped the pavement outside my apartment with the same tenacity clinging to his response.

Waiting a full day to tell him obviously hadn't made a difference. No amount of rest would've changed his mind.

"Walking down the aisle in a ceremony is one thing. But dancing? Sorry. Not gonna happen. He's not putting his frisky hands all over you."

I circled my arms around his back and tried to defuse him with a smile. "We'll be in a banquet hall, not some night club."

Riley cocked his head. "Like it matters to him."

"You're not giving him enough credit."

"Credit?" He untied my hands from around him. "That kind of went out the window when he didn't have enough integrity to stay away from an engaged girl while her fiancé was gone."

A stab of remorse struck my heart with another reminder of what our time apart had cost us. Was there any way to make it right?

"Maybe you'd feel better if you talked to him first—"

"I'd like to do a lot more than talk to him. And yeah, I'd feel loads better."

"Riley." I dipped my chin at him. "Aren't you supposed to be the mature one?"

His tense shoulders all but sneered at me.

Two girls carrying soccer balls stared at us from across the street.

I cinched my arms over my sides. "Please, just trust me."

A spark of the gentleness I loved about him touched his eyes. He swept my bangs away from my lashes. "It's not you I'm worried about."

Regardless of A. J.'s feelings toward me, he wouldn't do anything to jeopardize the perfect day Jaycee had planned. But this wasn't only about distrusting A. J.'s intentions. I'd hurt Riley more than he'd let on. The ache practically bled down his face.

"There's nothing A. J. can ever say or do to change my heart." Even though I'd messed up last semester, Riley had to know that was true.

The strain of doubt creasing his forehead crushed my heart. His eyes said everything he didn't have to. He wanted to let it go, wanted it to be okay, but it wasn't. And it was my fault.

Had he been stifling his resentment this whole time? All those hints of apprehension I'd seen shadow his face since he'd been back from Nashville... I wanted to pretend I hadn't seen them, that it was all behind us. But if he couldn't forgive me, where did that leave us now?

"Em..."

I backed up, turned. Knowing I couldn't outrun pain had never prevented my legs from trying. Halfway to the bridge, the downhill slope sent my entire body slamming into someone walking from the opposite direction.

"Whoa, is there a fire I don't know about?" Trevor's notorious grin filled every word.

I latched on to his arms to regain my balance but didn't look up from the concrete.

"Em? What's wrong?"

I tried to shoulder past him. "Nothing."

"You know the problem with lying to one of your friends?" He scanned from side to side and lowered his voice to a whisper. "We can tell."

"I'm fine."

"Mm-hmm." He tossed an arm around my shoulders and lugged me over to the knee-high brick ledge bordering the sidewalk. "Talk to me."

"Trev, I'm not in the mood."

Ignoring me, he rubbed his hands together. "Dang, it's cold out. You feel that ice seeping into your bones? I'd sure hate to have to stay out here any longer than we have to." He leaned his bulky shoulder into mine. "The sooner you start talking, the sooner we can go."

I craned my neck to the sky. Sometimes I hated having a brother-away-from-home.

He batted his eyes, waiting.

I exhaled. "It's this whole thing with Riley and A. J." I kicked my heel into the bricks. "I'm such an idiot for messing this up. You should've seen A. J.'s face when I went to see him the other day. He stopped going to the center because of me. And now, Riley's blowing up. I thought he'd let it go. Thought we were moving forward." Was this the real reason he was putting off his tour? Because he didn't trust me to wait for him?

Trevor blinked when I finally took a breath. "Is that all?"

He caught my hand before I could get up to walk away. "Kidding." His humor drained into one of his rare pensive expressions as he drew me into a side hug. "Now's not the time to lose heart. Not after everything you guys have been through. Love's enough, Em. Remember?"

Squeezed into his side, I closed my eyes and grasped on to that assurance.

He bobbed his shoulder against my cheek. His capacity to handle sentimental moments lasted only so long. "I think this calls for a night out with your friends."

"Does it include Starbucks?"

"Have you met my fiancée?" He towed me up from the ledge. "I'll even let you tell her it was your idea."

You'd think after almost four years, I wouldn't still be surprised at his ability to lighten any moment.

Another car occupied the spot where Riley's had been parked a little while ago. Knowing him, he'd left to give me the space he thought I needed.

Following right behind me, Trevor shut our apartment door and flaunted a grin at Jaycee. "Look who I found wandering around campus like a lost puppy."

I shoved him and headed for the teapot on the stove.

Jaycee tossed a dish towel over her shoulder. "Better a puppy than a stray. You should've seen her when she first got home from break."

I spun around, mouth slack. "Way to come to my rescue."

She hooked an arm around Trev. "What are friends for?"

I shook my head at them but couldn't keep a straight face. Cheaters. It wasn't fair for their laughter to be so contagious.

"See," Trevor said. "Told you all you needed was a night with your friends."

"Whatever would I do without you guys?"

Should've known better than to ask a loaded question. Jaycee and Trevor exchanged a mischievous glance. Thankfully, someone knocked on the door before either had a chance to beat the other to the punch line.

Even though our earlier conversation had ended in turmoil, relief swept in the second I saw Riley outside the door.

Until the look on his face nearly knocked me backward.

"What's wrong?"

Riley stared at the floor and gripped the trim like it was the only thing holding him in place. "Jasmine. She's…"

My heart hammered. "She's what?"

Without moving, he lifted his eyes to mine. "She's gone."

15

PIERCING

It took a minute for Riley's comment to register. I pulled him into the apartment. "What do you mean she's gone? Where? What happened?"

He strode into the entryway with both sets of fingers clasped through the back of his hair. "She ran away. No one knows where she is."

"Are the cops looking for her?"

"They're at the house now, but it's taking too long. She's diabetic. If she doesn't have food with her..." He stopped midstream, let his arms fall, and stared at the door. "I have to go. I have to find her."

"Wait." I caught the edge of his pullover as he turned. "Give me a sec. I'm coming with you."

I snatched the backpack leaning against the side of the couch and rushed to my bedroom to grab some extra clothes. Back in the kitchen, I scrambled for a couple bottles of water. "Did your parents check the tree house?"

No response.

I peered above the refrigerator door and winced. Of course they did. "Sorry. That was a stupid question." I hustled back over. "I'm sure they've looked everywhere they could think of."

Trev tossed me a flashlight. "Just in case."

Jaycee looped her arm around Trevor's. "Be careful."

"Thank you," I mouthed to both of them as I trailed Riley into the stairwell.

Outside, dark clouds blanketed the campus in a continuous shadow.

Riley thrust the car into gear before I yanked my door shut. I clicked my seat belt in with more force than necessary. "Where are we going? I mean, we can't just drive across the state looking for her?"

His knuckles whitened over the steering wheel.

Way to keep stating the obvious, Em.

"Sorry," I said again. I set a hand on his knee the way he had when I was freaking out about Austin. "We'll find her."

He threaded his fingers through mine.

Whatever we'd left unresolved earlier didn't matter right now. Riley needed me with him, and I'd go wherever that meant.

Staring ahead, he lurched the car into fourth gear. "Tell me she didn't."

Huh? "Didn't what?"

"I don't know why I didn't think about this before." He whipped around a semi into the left-hand lane. "I have a feeling I know where Jasmine went."

"Where?"

"I used to sneak out to these woods when Dad and I had a fight." The wipers sputtered across the drizzled-on windshield. "There's this little cave tucked away in the back. You can't even get to it without scaling a tree that's over the ravine." He shook his head. "It was the perfect hideout."

His smile fell. "I was so mad the night I caught Jazz following me." He twisted the wipers up another notch. "It's one thing for me to be out on my own. I can take care of myself. She's just a little girl. There are all kinds of animals and who-knows-what-else in those woods."

"I'm sure she's fine."

"What if she's not?" He banged his fist on the wheel. "I never should've gone home over Christmas."

"This isn't your fault. Riley, look at me." I lifted a hand to his cheek.

He glanced away from the road long enough to lock on to the assurance in my eyes.

"Jazz is one clever girl," I said. "I think you might be surprised at how well she can take care of herself. I doubt there's a tree she can't master."

An overdue exhale seeped out. "You're probably right. She's been climbing trees since she was old enough to stand."

"And if there are any animals naive enough to chase her," I teased, "she's probably already won them over."

A gentle laugh lowered Riley's shoulders the rest of the way. He smoothed his thumb over the back of my hand. "Thanks."

I settled in my seat. Honestly, the rift between Riley and his dad very well could've been the reason Jasmine ran away. It seemed to affect her more than the others. But I had to believe she'd be okay and that we'd find her. There simply wasn't another option.

The miles passed much faster than the first time we drove them. Riley parked in front of what looked like a lake. His headlights tunneled into the fog rising between a series of pine trees.

With the engine off, it wasn't hard to understand why he'd turned here for peace. The sounds of the forest blended into a lullaby I could've fallen asleep to under different circumstances. Not to mention the fragrance. The trees might as well have been growing hundreds of Yankee candles instead of pinecones.

"This way," he called from a few strides ahead of me.

Holding the flashlight between my teeth, I zipped my book bag and looped my arms through the straps. I jogged up the path, dodging overgrown roots, until I was less than a foot behind him.

The deeper the shadows grew, the further they eroded the serenity that had felt indestructible only a few minutes ago. Instead of a collective symphony, each sound echoed on its own. I glanced toward every noise, hyper aware of our intrusion into the night's normal routine.

Something howled. We both froze.

"Riley?" I reached for his hand.

A scream more piercing than any howl shook through the trees.

Riley took off in a sprint. Underbrush clawed at my ankles as I ran after him. "Riley, wait." Wind scraped down my lungs. Overgrown branches whipped across my cheeks, but I didn't slow down until the trail split. I spun in a circle. No sight of Riley, only fog. I stopped moving, stopped breathing, and listened for any clue on which way to go.

Another howl.

I whirled toward the sound and ran. A sharp corner sent me stumbling into Riley.

He steadied me by the waist. "Don't move," he whispered.

Adrenaline-fueled breaths came hard and sharp, the cold air burning in my chest.

He turned off the flashlight and steered my eyes toward an animal prowling close to the ground a stone's throw away.

"Is that...?"

"A wolf."

Didn't wolves travel in packs? Panic set right back in. I wanted to shrink into the darkness, run to the car. We had to get out of there. "Riley, we need to—"

He put a finger to his lips and pointed at a cave on the

other side of some type of gully. A long, curvy branch from a tree rooted on our side of the woods nearly barricaded the entire face of the cave. Something moved behind the leaves. Moonlight filtered through the trees onto a panic-ridden Jasmine, standing flush against the inside wall.

The wolf clawed at the edge of the cliff. Riley inched forward. I grabbed his shoulders. "No." Even with a running start, there was no way he'd clear the jump.

"It's the cooler." He flicked his chin toward it. "Jazz has food with her. The wolf's too distracted to notice me."

"Jazz?" Melody yelled from the trail right before flying straight into me. When did she get here?

Riley didn't flinch. "Stay back, Mel."

Without acknowledging him, she sprang up the maple tree beside us.

Riley shot to his feet. "What are you doing?"

She scaled the arced branch like it was nothing and landed on the ground beside her sister. The *thump* echoed in the cave, followed by a menacing growl. Both girls gasped. The wolf spotted the tree and snarled.

Riley hedged me into the woods, out of view, and turned to the cave. "Mel, look at me." His voice held an assurance I had no idea how he was maintaining. "When I say go, you take Jazz back up that tree. Don't move until I say so. Do you understand me?"

Acknowledging Riley for the first time, Melody nodded.

"On three." He snagged a large rock from the ground. "One..."

I followed his eyes toward the wolf circling the tree trunk. "What are you doing?"

"Two..."

He inched closer, crouched.

"Riley, no..."

"Three."

Melody flung Jasmine onto the branch at the same time Riley dove on top of the wolf. He raised the rock, but the wolf knocked it free with his snout. The animal flipped over and sank its teeth into Riley's arm. Jasmine screamed even louder than he did.

I dropped to my knees in search of something—another rock, anything. The wolf towered above him with his paws pinned to his chest. A vicious snarl shuddered across the ground and up my body. Riley looked at me with eyes carrying more of a burden than they ever should have. The stone I'd grabbed rolled out of my hand.

Everything stopped until a deafening noise retriggered time and motion again.

The wolf snapped his head in the direction of the gunshot and tore off, nicking Riley's face as he went. Leaves rustled behind me. Mrs. Preston rushed up and left her husband standing twenty feet away with a rifle still raised against his shoulder blade.

She fell beside Riley and checked him over, fear and relief colliding.

"I'm fine," he said.

Jasmine landed on the ground. "Riley, I'm so sorry. I didn't mean for—"

"What were you thinking, young lady?" Mrs. Preston tugged Jazz into her arms.

I bolted over, dug out an extra shirt I'd packed, and tied it around Riley's arm. Leaves crunched under footsteps creeping up from behind us. A glance at Mr. Preston's boots trailed up to his face, calm and collected, under the broken moonlight.

Jasmine rose to her feet. "I'm sorry, Mom, but I couldn't take it anymore." From the center of the group, she turned toward each of us. Her flare of indignation bled into sorrow when she stopped in front of Mr. Preston. "He's a part of our family, Dad. You can't keep pretending he's not." She faced Riley. "Please. Please try to find a way to remember you love him."

She shuffled in a circle in front of her family, eyes beseeching.

No one spoke. Even the trees seemed breathless. Every sound bowed to a silence dedicated to the earnestness in this little girl's heart.

Mrs. Preston searched her son over once more. He nodded again that he was fine.

Looking from him to her husband, she stretched her arms around her two daughters. "C'mon, girls. They'll meet us at home. *After* they stop at the clinic," she said, staring at Riley.

I helped him to his feet. Leaning on my shoulder,

Riley stumbled forward until he regained a sense of balance.

Mr. Preston stepped in front of us, face unreadable. He placed a firm hand on Riley's shoulder, extended the other, and looked his son in the eye. "Thank you."

I'd heard those two words spoken by countless people on countless occasions. But in that moment, it was more than an everyday phrase. It was the beginning of a reconciliation that everyone except a ten-year-old girl had lost hope in ever seeing.

16

GRACE

After stopping for stitches and a rabies shot, we made it back to the Preston's in time to see the cops pulling away. Inside, a welcome and natural sound of family filled their small dining room.

Something had changed. His dad sat with us for hours, quiet but at ease. He leaned against the table as he rose and extended an all-encompassing good night to the rest of us. Jasmine bounced on Mrs. Preston's lap, as if she hadn't been in any danger that evening whatsoever.

Riley and I exchanged a glance across the table, both shaking our heads until a gradual silence hushed over the room. I followed Mrs. Preston's gaze toward the hollow doorway where Melody slumped into the frame while removing her earphones. She looked younger somehow, more tender.

Mrs. Preston scooted Jasmine off her lap. "C'mon, sweetie. I think it's about time we get you in bed."

"But Mom—"

"Come on, now. Off you go." She hurried Jazz out of the room.

The old Lab hobbled after them as they disappeared down the hallway. One look between Riley and Melody made it clear I should've followed.

Melody stepped forward at the same time Riley and I both rose from the table.

I stopped halfway out of my chair. If shrinking under the table wouldn't have brought even more attention to myself, I probably would've done it. I sank back into my seat instead. Maybe they'd pretend I wasn't there.

Melody fidgeted with her earphones and glanced intermittently between Riley and her feet. The quiet house accentuated every tiny noise until she finally spoke. "You left us."

His chin drooped to his chest. "I know. Mel, I—"

"It's cool to call me Melody." The slightest smile touched her voice. "I sort of miss hearing you say it."

Repentance tore down his face when he reached her side.

I twisted the bottom of the tablecloth, wringing back the blasted tears that being here somehow always stirred.

"I'm sorry, Melody."

Still dawdling in the doorway, she lowered her gaze. "Just don't ever do it again, okay?"

He laughed softly. "Okay."

"Okay," she repeated in a way that settled things.

It had to be the most awkward and understated reconciliation I'd ever seen, but Melody had done it in her own way. And that had made it even more sincere.

She dragged her socks across the hardwood floor on her way down the hall.

There were so many things I wanted to say, but I simply smiled at Riley. Anything left unsaid could wait until morning.

He led me to his bedroom door and kissed my cheek.

I grabbed his hand. "Let me take the couch tonight. You're injured."

"Injured?" His grin tipped sideways. "You make it sound like I was in a car wreck or something."

"Oh, sorry. I forgot having a wrestling match with a wolf fits in the no-big-deal category."

"It's nothing, I promise. I'll be fine." He took one look at the way I perched my fist on my hip in disagreement and laughed. "If my mom wakes up to find you on the couch, *then* I might seriously be injured."

"Way to play the Mom-card." *Cheater.* "Fine. But I'm driving tomorrow."

He drew me close. "Deal."

With another kiss good night, I left Riley in the hall, groped my way through the cluttered room, and climbed into his old twin-size bed. I wouldn't have any trouble resting this time. The combination of emotional and physical exhaustion was bound to create the perfect tonic for a dreamless sleep. Tomorrow would be another story.

IN CAHOOTS with the alarm clock, sunshine climbed across the floor, pooled over the wrinkled covers, and landed on the nightstand. I swatted the obnoxious clock before it could wake up the entire house.

Riley and I needed to have words about his leave-at-the-crack-of-dawn plan. I appreciated that he wanted to get me back with plenty of time to prep for the start of the semester. Still, I wasn't sure being a zombie was going to help.

I grabbed the towel Mrs. Preston had left for me and crept into the hall. Light from under the bathroom door cast a solid beam down the floor. Riley must've beaten me to the shower. I hung my towel on the handle and headed to the kitchen for a glass of water while I waited.

It took less than two steps into the dining room for the aroma of baking bread to lure my body the rest of the way without any prompting.

No surprise, Mrs. Preston was stirring in the kitchen already. If the fresh powder residue on the front of her apron was any indication, she'd been up for some time.

"Good morning." She hovered over an open cookbook. "Can I get you something to drink, dear? I just brewed a fresh pot of coffee."

"Oh, um, water's fine, please. Thank you."

She straightened and stared at me over a narrow pair of reading glasses like I'd spoken in a foreign language. She flittered over to the refrigerator, poured a glass of orange juice instead, and handed it to me.

"I know Riley's bent on leaving early this morning, but you can't go without having a decent breakfast first." She refilled her coffee mug.

It didn't matter how short of a time I'd known her. I'd seen that same determined look a thousand times from her son. The invitation to breakfast wasn't negotiable.

She motioned for me to have a seat at the small kitchen table in the corner.

I drew one leg onto a chair cushion covered in a decorative rooster pattern and rubbed the dog's back with my other foot.

Mrs. Preston consumed her coffee with almost as much reverence as Jaycee did. No wonder she'd looked at me like I was crazy when I'd passed on having some myself.

"Thanks for coming yesterday." She fretted with the corner of her glasses. "I don't know what that girl was thinking. Leave it to Jasmine to be theatrical in making a point." Her smile betrayed her tone of reprimand. "She's always been our scare-child. Gave us quite a good one a couple years ago. Ended up in the hospital with insulin shock."

I'd forgotten Riley had mentioned she was diabetic. "How did you know where to find her?"

"Melody." Mrs. Preston set her coffee on the placemat. "She remembered overhearing Jasmine refer to that park as some kind of secret hideout." She stared at the wall beside me, probably reliving memories she'd rather erase. "I'm so thankful Riley thought to search there too."

"I'd say he's just as lucky you all got there when you did. That wolf..." I shuddered at the possibility of how much more damage he could've done.

She traced her finger along her mug handle. "Oh, I think Riley might've given him a run for his money. My boy has a lot of fight in him."

"So I'm learning." Getting to see new dimensions of Riley's personality reminded me of the way Dad used to refer to love—a journey of exploration. That journey would lead us to marriage eventually, wouldn't it? Despite all the obstacles and delays?

I willed back the doubt creeping through my rib cage. "Mrs. Preston?" I cleared my throat. "Riley and I haven't finalized our wedding plans, but it would mean so much to us both if Mr. Preston would be there."

I kept my eyes on the pulp in my cup. "Actually, it's more than just wanting him there. Do you think...? I mean, I know Riley and his dad still have stuff to work through, and he has some reservations about us getting married, but do you think he'll give us his blessing?" I would've been surprised if she'd heard the last five words. The weight of what they meant nearly crushed the sound of my voice altogether.

A smile curved around the brim of her mug. No

guessing whom Riley had inherited his eyes of assurance from.

Her expression turned wistful as she straightened the wire napkin holder in the center of the table. "We were just kids when we got married. I was only nineteen. Jonathan was full of dreams. I would've followed him anywhere. *Did* follow him anywhere." She laughed before taking another lengthy drink. Steam rose from the mug and fogged her glasses.

"Life's been hard on him, Emma. Riley thinks he understands, but he doesn't know the extent Jonathan's disappointments reach. He was always such a private man. Sometimes too private. I'm afraid he didn't let Riley into some of the places of his heart that he should've."

"Is it too late?"

She abandoned her mug long enough to set an affirming hand over mine. "It's never too late, dear."

Would that same grace extend to Riley's career? If he wouldn't listen to me, maybe he'd respond to his mom. I twisted my hair over my shoulder. "Would you talk to Riley about touring? Try to help him see what he's sacrificing?"

She sat back. "Have I mentioned my son's stubborn like his father?"

It had to be worth a try.

Riley appeared in the doorway and stumbled over to the oven in the same sweet-aroma-driven trance I had earlier. "I see you didn't listen to me, Mom," he mumbled with a mouthful of warm bread.

"I see you're disappointed." Mrs. Preston's grin was just as wry as his.

I downed the rest of my orange juice to keep from laughing. The more time I spent with her, the more she captured my heart. Same with the rest of his family.

Riley opened the fridge. "No six pack?"

"Your dad doesn't drink like he used to." She squeezed my hand on her way up from her seat and started serving Riley a homemade meal before he sat down. "Not everything's the same, dear."

Sure hoped that was true.

I kissed his cheek and headed for the bathroom.

A shower might've tamed my hair, but traces of my conversation with Mrs. Preston kept my insides in a jumbled mess. Or maybe it was knowing I had to say goodbye to a family I already felt a part of.

The Prestons formed a half-circle around us in front of the Civic. Mrs. Preston turned from Riley to me. "Take care of my boy." Without the slightest hesitation, she closed me in a hug I hated to release. She leaned back and held my arms a minute longer, a heartwarming smile barely restraining the beginning of tears.

Riley drew her tight. "Don't worry, Mom. We'll visit again soon."

I tucked my hands in my pockets and lowered my chin at the sight of Mr. Preston stepping forward. A few hours of being at ease with him last night wasn't enough to know where he stood. I stared at the decorative pavement, stalling. As if the awkwardness couldn't get any worse, he extended a hand toward me in a delayed reaction.

I shook it and matched his silence with a tentative smile.

"Finish strong," he said.

School was the furthest thing from my mind right then. I thought he disapproved of my field of study, but there was no mistaking the encouragement in his charge.

He turned to his son. I bit my lip, hopeful and terrified at the same time. I was so focused on hearing the words about to leave his mouth, I didn't even see Jasmine coming. Engulfed by two short arms winding around my waist, I staggered backward.

"I miss you already," Jasmine said with a sniffle.

Forcing down the lump in my throat, I unwound myself from her hug and grabbed both her hands. "You have a very busy few months ahead of you."

She tilted her head to one side, looking puzzled.

I leaned in closer to disclose her covert assignment. "Just think of all the stores you'll have to visit until you find the perfect flower girl dress."

Her eyes lit up with the thrill of a newly acquired mission.

I turned in time to see Mr. Preston releasing Riley's hand. I'd missed what they'd said to each other, but the looks on their faces made it clear words weren't needed.

Riley strung his arm across my shoulders. "Ready?"

"Wait!"

Everyone in the driveway spun toward a sleep-tousled version of Melody, yelling from the front door. She hustled down the driveway and ran straight into Riley's arms. "You're coming back, right? I mean, some-time soon?"

"I promised, remember?" Riley hugged her in a final seal of his word.

She caught my gaze.

I thought saying goodbye to Mr. Preston was awkward, but this might've been worse. Not that I could blame her for slanting me a wary stare. I probably would've done the same if it were Austin. She had a gentle side under her cover though. You just had to know how to find it.

"Maybe we can talk sometime." I tore out a slip of paper from inside my purse and jotted down my cell number and email address. "I need some help picking out music for the wedding."

"Really?" she said, struggling to keep her tone dry.

"Yeah, definitely. You can email me some of your ideas."

Melody glanced around our small circle before looking back at me. "Cool."

The genuine smile that followed might not have meant we were officially best friends, but I'd take what I could get.

As Riley and I drove off, their reflection shrank in the rearview mirror and dissolved around the corner.

Riley flashed an elusive grin at me from the passenger's seat.

I flaunted it right back. "What?"

"Nothing."

Nothing. Right. "I know that smile."

It stretched all the wider. "Then you know what I'm thinking."

"That you drive me crazy sometimes?"

He laughed. "Glad I'm not the only one going mad around here. Though, I doubt for the same reason." He tilted his head back against the headrest. "You sure you don't want to elope on the way home? There's gotta be a church nearby."

I shook my head at him. "How 'bout you concentrate on taking a nap instead. All the fatigue is catching up to you."

"Pretty sure it's that I'm falling even more in love with you." He curled his fingertips under mine.

I kept my eyes on the road but couldn't shake the smile from my face to save my life. Good thing churches didn't show up on exit signs like gas stations did. *Just keep driving.*

PARKED in front of my apartment, I stretched out my back. "I think it's safe to classify that as the most eventful break of my college career."

Instead of laughing with me, Riley kept his eyes on

his lap, his thoughts obviously tied up in something else. "Em, about the other day…"

I unbuckled my seat belt. "I'll tell Jaycee the dance is out. She'll understand." I picked at a snag on the bottom of the steering wheel. "But I need to know. The reason you're not touring… Is it because you're worried we won't make it apart? Is that why you want to move up the wedding?"

He didn't lift his head. "I'm ready to spend every day of my life with you, Emma Matthews. At any cost."

I felt the same way, but he didn't have to sacrifice one for the other. "I'm sorry I let the distance come between us last time. I was scared, afraid of losing you. But not anymore." I reached across the seats and squeezed his hand. "I trust this, and I just want you to do the same."

"I do." A long blink lifted his eyes toward mine and reinforced all the promises he'd ever made me.

"Then, please, don't jeopardize your future because of fear. I know you resent your dad's choices and don't want to repeat them, but if you give up because of me, you'll end up resenting me too." Couldn't he see that?

"I'm not giving up my dream." He twisted in his seat. "I'm going to tour. Just later."

"But Nick—"

"Nick's a businessman. He knows how to heap on the pressure, but he knows when to fold too. There's no way he's backing out of this investment."

Maybe so, but it wasn't only about him. "You're sure

144 | CRYSTAL WALTON

this isn't about trust? You're not putting the tour on hold because of A. J.?"

Riley rubbed a thumb over the backs of my fingers. "I'm not gonna pretend I don't wonder what you feel when you're with him, but you're right. I have to let it go."

Swallowing, I searched for words to erase any doubt in his mind.

"This isn't a question of your commitment. It's my own battle. And I'm not going to ruin Jaycee's wedding day because I'm jealous." His grin slanted. "But... I might have to cut in as soon as the first dance is over."

I dished his sassy grin back at him. "Promise?"

A slow kiss answered for him.

And I was supposed to focus on school after that? Or on anything else, period? Maybe Vegas wasn't such a bad idea. I'd probably been overcomplicating things. Trev was right. Love was enough. We'd work through everything else.

If life would slow down for at least a week, maybe we could actually think straight and figure this out. Sleep couldn't hurt either.

I grabbed my bag and stepped halfway out of the car. "You want to come up?"

My eyes must've hinted the thousand pleases tacked on to the end of my question. Despite the exhausted look on his face, he nodded and followed me up to my apartment.

Visions of crashing onto my bed beside him for a

much-needed nap welcomed me at the door. Prepping for classes could wait. After this crazy trip, we were definitely due a little breather.

One step inside killed that possibility. Trevor, Jaycee, and A. J. all swung their heads in our direction. Riley and I stopped in the doorway. A. J. scooted to the edge of the couch, straightened his jeans, and slumped back again like he couldn't decide whether to sit or stand.

In a matter of seconds, Jaycee and I had an entire conversation through nothing but facial expressions. She elbowed Trevor to intervene, but A. J. tossed a throw pillow aside and hopped to his feet before Trevor got a word out.

"Trev told me what happened." A. J. started toward us. "I came by to make sure everything was okay."

"Everything's fine. We found Jasmine." I lowered my bag to the floor, thankful my jaw decided to work again. "She's safe. Just a little audacious." And impossible not to forgive.

Jaycee exhaled. "Thank God. I tried to call you, like, ten times yesterday."

"Yeah, sorry. It was kind of a crazy night." And morning. With everything on my mind, I hadn't even thought to call her on the way home. I glanced back at Riley.

Apparently, I wasn't the only one with jaw problems. He looked like the tin man, waiting for someone to oil his joints. Either he was trying not to relive memories from last night, or he was trying to restrain himself from decking A. J. in the face. I couldn't tell which.

Trevor must've been on the same page. He crept forward, as if gearing up to intercept a potential brawl.

A. J. paused in front of us with his head down, and then passed through without a word. Riley remained perfectly still. He might not have completely let go yet, but at least he was trying. I angled in front of him to meet his eyes.

The shell of a grin pushed through his tight muscles. "One day at a time."

With all that was still ahead of us, that was probably all any of us could handle.

17

CHOICES

THE BUSY START to the semester hadn't kept my heart away from the center. After rearranging my shift around my new course schedule, I finally made it back to the office and back to the fight I wasn't about to give up on. The clock could tick on to the end of February all it wanted. We still had a month and a half to beat it.

Other than an increased pile of papers in my inbox, my desk hadn't been disturbed over the break. Too bad I couldn't say the same about the "For Rent" sign still posted on the door. If refraining from tearing it down when I came in hadn't proven Trey's perspective mantra was rubbing off on me, I'm not sure what would have.

I thumbed through the mail. No new leads on grant requests. Figured. What I'd do to be able to rewind time to last semester and—

Last semester. My pulse jumped at the thought. It'd

probably be a long shot, but what if Jim Brake wasn't with the Success Foundation anymore? Even if he was, the organization had been interested in supporting us originally. Maybe he didn't have the final say.

I opened my contact spreadsheet, scrolled to their office number, and grabbed my phone.

A woman answered the line. "Thank you for calling the Success Foundation, how may I assist you?"

Good question. I wound the cord around my finger. "Um, Finance, please?"

"Mr. Chandler or Da Silva?"

Anyone but Mr. Brake. "Whoever's in charge." *Might as well go straight to the top.*

"May I ask who's calling?"

The memory of Mr. Brake and his wife stopping by the center that time clipped into my side. She worked there, too, didn't she? What if she was on the other end of the line right now? After how worked up he'd gotten when he'd accused Dee of breaking into his daughter's car, he would likely never let her forget us.

Holding in a breath, I snagged a pencil and scrambled for a way to deflect any connection to the center in case she knew who I was. "Emma Preston." Close enough.

"Hold, please."

I flipped the pencil between my fingers while waiting for someone to pick up.

Neal Chandler's voicemail kicked in. I sat up and cleared my throat. "Yes, Mr. Chandler, this is Emma from the Downtown Portland Center. You may remember offering us a provisional grant a few months ago."

I pushed down a dry swallow and dug deep for confidence. "I'm afraid personal matters might've influenced Mr. Brake's decision to revoke the offer, and I'm calling to request another representative reconsider our proposal. I'll follow up with an email so we can work on the quickest resolution. Thank you for your time." I hung up and exhaled.

If Riley had been there, he would've flaunted one of his famous lawyer-looks at me. That business law class was bound to come in handy at some point. Hopefully, it'd pay off.

The classroom door opened a few minutes later. Trey tapped my desk on his way toward his own. "Welcome back."

"Thanks. Glad to be home. What'd I miss?"

"Oh, you know. The usual." He bottomed out in his chair. "Teneecia almost cut off all her sister's braids on Friday. Parker decided to turn the classroom wall into an art project. And Andre managed to instigate a mass battle of the sexes on the basketball court."

I laughed so hard I snorted. "Never a dull moment."

"Ain't that the truth?" He stretched his chair back as far as it would go and flashed a look of insanity across his face. "How was your break away from all the chaos here?"

"Um… let's just say, I'd take the chaos here any day."

He sloped his glasses down his nose and looked at me for an explanation.

"Don't ask." I wouldn't have known where to start anyway. So much had happened. Being back at the center felt like pushing a reset button. As crazy as things were, life made sense here.

The conversation I'd had with Mr. Preston around the dinner table the first night we were at their house came flooding back. Our work here was far more than charity.

"Mm-hmm." Trey grunted.

I blinked. "What?"

"I don't think you're fully back from your trip."

"Sorry." I shuffled some papers around. "I'm here. Promise."

"Well, that's good. Because in about five seconds, you'll have no choice." He looked at his watch and pointed to the door leading to the classroom. "In five… four… three… two… one."

On perfect cue, the door swung open. A stampede of kids gushed out with enough noise to pass for a marching band.

"Miss E. Miss E. You're back!"

A group of girls almost knocked my chair over, trying to climb onto my lap.

"Missed you, too, girls." More than I'd realized.

Tania finally won the battle and secured her spot in my lap. She could've been a younger Jasmine. They were about the same build. Both carried an energetic and contagious drive. Except I didn't know if anyone was at home to shower Tania in the same affection Mrs. Preston gave Jasmine. But if we offered her even a fraction of it here, then our work at the center wasn't a waste. It'd carry on, even if we closed. Wouldn't it? Somehow? The question ached without an answer.

"Okay, girls." Trey headed over. "Let's give Miss E some breathing room." He lifted Tania off my lap and prodded them all toward the basketball court. "I bet there are some rowdy boys out back waiting for a rematch."

That did it. A split-second glance flitted between the girls before they scampered through the door to the competition awaiting them on the court. If the stack of paperwork looming on my desk weren't glaring at me, I would've joined them.

The front door creaked open. Two of our younger girls tiptoed through the office while eyeing Trey in a game he probably had no idea he was playing. As soon as he peered up from his desk, the girls blazed through the screen door with a trail of giggles following them.

After the third time they'd snuck back through, Trey's expression pushed my grin into outright laughter. I hid my face behind a piece of paper when the sound of the front door opening signaled yet another round of the girls' endless entertainment.

Trey rose to his feet but made no warning. In fact, he

made no sound at all. I peeked above the page and dropped it.

For the briefest moment, I would've sworn I was looking into Dee's eyes again. "Ms. Mendierez?"

Instead of the disillusioned, frayed woman I'd seen in her house, a composed and neatly manicured one met me now. Her short-sleeved button-up shirt and apron bore the trademarks of one of the local diners.

She turned to Trey. "I'm sorry if I'm interrupting. I came to see Miss Matthews."

He nodded with perception. "It's about time for me to go check on our little warriors out back. Those boys don't know what they're up against."

He closed us in a room weighed with silence. Ms. Mendierez fiddled with the edge of her apron. "I'm on my way to work." One hesitant step forward turned into a determined stride across the room. "Miss Matthews—"

"Emma," I said. "Please, call me Emma."

"Emma, I came by to thank you." She stared at her feet. "When I lost Dee, I thought I lost my reason for living. But I was wrong." She released her apron and raised her head. "Someone may have stolen my boy's chance to live his dreams, but ain't nobody gonna take away my chance to honor them for him."

Instead of bitterness or vengeance, conviction colored her eyes. She studied me as though I was a tangible connection to her son. "Thank you," she whispered. "Dee isn't the only one you taught to be courageous."

A ball of emotions claimed my voice.

She backed up and blinked away her tears. "Did you find out anything about the possibility of selling his artwork?"

"Actually, I just gave some samples to my brother to pass on to his connections. I'm hoping to hear from him in the next couple of weeks. Once we have a buyer, I'll put him in contact with you."

"That's great." She stood tall and collected in front of me. "I'd like to donate fifty percent of any proceeds to the center." She shook her head. "I know it might not be much, but I believe it's what Dee would've wanted."

"Ms. Mendierez—"

"No arguments." She smoothed out her apron. "Now, then, Trey mentioned something about having classes here for adults."

"That's right," Trey said from the doorway. "And you're just in time to start our class on financial management. I think you might like the teacher." He brandished a telling grin my way.

He couldn't be serious. "Me?"

He sauntered over. "I seem to recall you being interested in teaching this class when you first started here."

"Yeah, when I was gullible enough to let you talk me into it." And before the center was on the verge of closing. What was the point now?

He waved off my response and turned to Ms. Mendierez. "The class starts next week."

I latched on to his forearm for balance.

He chuckled. "Or maybe a few weeks from now."

Or a few years.

Ms. Mendierez drew her keys from her pocket. "Sounds great. I should be going. My shift starts in fifteen." She glanced from Trey to me. "Thank you both. I'll be in touch."

She'd reached the door before my brain fog cleared long enough to remember I had something for her. "Wait." I snagged Dee's journal from my desk drawer and jogged over. "I'm sorry it's taken me so long to return this. When you're ready, I've bookmarked a page for you to read."

I handed her the journal and squeezed her arm. "It's easy to see why Dee looked up to you as a strong, courageous woman. You're much braver than you think you are."

She cradled the journal close to her chest and looked away. Glassy but determined eyes found mine again a moment later. "Thank you, Emma. For everything."

I smiled back, and she trekked outside toward a chance to prove me right.

Truth was, none of us really understood the courage we had until the moment we needed it most. Winter break had made that clear. How much more courage would the rest of the year require? And how was I this close to finishing college to begin with?

I didn't want to think about that or whether I was ready to teach a class. I didn't want to worry about when Riley and I would get married or wonder where life would take us after February. I only wanted to live right here and now.

I rolled my chair up to my desk and faced my work head-on. *One day at a time.*

IT WAS seven o'clock before I uncovered the bottom of my inbox. No telling when it had last seen daylight. As I extended my arms behind my head, my outdated desk chair tilted backward much farther than it was ever designed to.

Trey was still busy crunching numbers on a piece of paper under his desk lamp. Even the shadows couldn't hide the worn creases lining his face. Poor guy needed some rest.

If it weren't for that stupid incident with Tito last semester, Trey might've felt comfortable leaving me here alone. Those carefree days were long gone. It didn't seem fair for Tito's impact to be lingering still. Maybe if I talked to him, got him to back off whatever pressure he was putting on Mr. Glyndon, things could be different.

"I'll be ready in a few minutes, Trey." I clambered from my chair toward the back door.

He peeked up from his desk but didn't say anything.

I flung my coat over my shoulders on my way outside. Amazing how things could transform in a matter of hours. Distant traffic hummed in place of animated voices and shuffling sneakers. Instead of little arms and legs pulling at my sides, the stillness in the air closed around me and collected each exhale.

The outdoor light shined over the ragged basketball net at the opposite end of the court—one more mark of Tito's recklessness. Not that the rundown court was anything less than what the kids expected. But they shouldn't have to accept things just because that was how they'd always been.

On the stone bench, I ran my fingertips across the empty spot where Dee had sat with me months before. Peering at the stars, I tucked the sides of my coat into each other to block the wind from coursing through me.

We couldn't lose everything. This place. The work we'd done here. It was supposed to matter. It was supposed to make a difference that would last.

Dee's voice raced to mind like it always did when I faltered. "*I am courageous.*"

I breathed in knowing I couldn't let that courage be for nothing. There had to be a way. I faced the sky again, begging for direction.

"It's peaceful, isn't it?" Trey said from the door.

He strolled over to join me. With his arms folded across his stomach, he surveyed the vacant court. This was as much a home to him as it was to the kids.

"You know, I was thinking." I angled toward him. "What if we put together an event to raise funds for the center? Make it a service day and get the kids involved. They might not all have talents like Dee, but they each have something to offer. I want to help them see that."

If we had to close, at least they could take that truth with them.

The light cast a shadow of Trey's grin over the bench.

I scrunched my lips to the side. "You think I'm crazy, don't you?"

"Oh, quite the contrary. I think you're much wiser than your years."

Since when did wrestling with doubt make you wise? I dragged the tips of my Converse sneakers along the pavement under the bench. "Do you ever wonder if what you're doing is worthwhile?"

"I think we all do at some point." He adjusted his newsboy cap and leaned against the bricks behind us. "Wanting answers isn't necessarily a bad thing. Sometimes—and I reckon it's more often than not in your case—questions are evidence your heart's in the right place. It's when we stop caring enough to ask questions that we end up losing our way."

"Mm-hmm," I grunted in classic Trey-style. "Spoken like a true sage."

He laughed his deep hearty laugh. "We're gonna miss you around here, kid."

"Hey, you're not rid of me yet." I clasped the bench, nowhere near ready to say goodbye.

We both looked out toward the court and held on to the quiet moment a little longer.

"There's always gonna be brokenness," he said softly. "Things that don't make sense, things we can't change. That doesn't mean we stop trying."

I swallowed back the tears that'd been threatening to break through all day. Time might've been against us. And we sure enough didn't have control over where the road led next, but at least we could choose to face each bend with hope—even the ones that tried to rob us of it.

"Trey?" I whispered. "I think it's time I visit Tito."

18

IMPRISONED

THE AIR outside the prison ward hovered on all sides of me like an invisible cell. Thick. Stagnant. The apprehension that had been building since last night hurled me back to the car. This was a mistake. I reached for the door.

"You've got this." Trey pried my fingers from the handle.

I held in a deep breath and exhaled. "Okay."

I strode beside him as he made his way through a small group of visitors congregated in front of the windowless wall to speak with a uniformed guard at the door. "Marcus, my man." He clasped the guard's hand. "We got, what? Like, five minutes to visiting hours? You really gonna keep us out in the cold like this, bro?"

"I don't make the rules, Williams." He rose from his stool, and I about tripped over my feet, backing up. Who was this guy? The Rock's brother? His square face could've been chiseled out of the cinder block behind him.

His size apparently didn't faze Trey. He kept messing with him like they were old friends. How many times had he come to visit Tito?

My pulse picked up again. I dwindled a little farther into the crowd, away from the door separating those on either side of it.

A shrill buzz rang into the air and up my shoulders. I swallowed hard when Trey motioned me inside. After only a few strides across the dingy white tiles, the door closed behind us. I flinched at the echo traveling down the full length of the dim hallway.

Trey prodded me forward again. I gripped his coat sleeve and leaned closer each time a musty draft streamed in from a side room manned by another guard.

He stopped each person at the door for some sort of screening before ushering them through the metal detector. I lifted on my toes to see around a burly woman in front of me. A small, square windowpane showed a glimpse inside.

In the far back corner, Tito glanced up from a table as if he felt me staring. One look. That was all it took. I fell back on my heels, chest tightening. Flashes of another scene poured in. Dee's broken body in my arms. Life draining without any way to stop it. Oceans of heartache. Drowning.

The hallway darkened. Trey's muffled voice trailed from beside the guard. I strained for balance but couldn't stand. Couldn't move. I caved against the wall. What was I doing here?

Trey secured his hand under my elbow. "You all right?" he whispered.

Blinks replaced words.

He signaled for the pair behind me to go ahead of us. Once they passed, he placed a hand on either of my shoulders and looked at me with the same encouragement that rarely left his eyes. "You can do this, Emma."

I rehearsed it to myself until a deep, calming breath brought everything back into focus. Straightening, I approached the checkpoint. *For Dee.*

The door buzzed us in. Several tables cluttered the small room, each with an inmate on one side and a visitor on the other. The prisoners' orange jumpsuits practically glowed against the dull gray backdrop.

I scanned the bleak walls, dodging the cameras, until the waning distance left me no choice but to look straight toward the table approaching too fast. Tito kept his chin dropped to his chest and his hands fidgeting on the tabletop. Without lifting his head, he looked up as we neared. Something in his eyes had changed. My gaze dashed to the floor.

His chair scraped the tiles as he met a half-hug-half-handshake from Trey.

Trey's unconditional acceptance never failed to catch me off guard. I seized the top of the chair in front of me. My clammy hands skimmed down the metal frame, but I managed to drag it out far enough to sit down.

Tito turned his back toward me and lowered his voice as he talked to Trey. Something about his kid brother. I probably didn't want to hear it anyway. Tito's recklessness had landed him in jail and Lucas in juvenile detention. Hadn't he caused enough damage? Why couldn't he leave the center alone?

At the table beside us, a little girl—maybe three years old—sat on a woman's lap. A shabby teddy bear hung from her pudgy fingers and draped over the floor. She stared at the man across from her. Probably her father. Though tears clung to the woman's lashes, the little girl's eyes remained vacant, as though struggling to place who this stranger was.

She could've been the younger sister of any of the kids at the center. Most likely would've been there herself at some point. If it weren't closing.

The ache of loss rushed in and shut the place out until Trey's voice cut through the white noise in the background. "I need to speak with the guard." He motioned toward the door. "I'll just leave you two alone."

Alone? He might as well have shouted it through a megaphone. The word kept rebounding in my ears with enough force to knock me over. I gripped the table edge. He patted my shoulder as he passed.

Tito sank onto his chair and stared at the table for a minute before meeting my eyes. "You's the last person I expected to see here, señorita."

That made two of us.

He tilted his chair backward and dragged his hands over his shaved head. I looked away. I couldn't do this.

His chair dropped onto all four legs. The sharp sound drew a glance from the guard, but he didn't move.

Tito lowered his head so far, his exhale left a momentary stain of breath on the metal surface. "I'm sorry," he said. "For hurtin' you."

My arms slid off the table onto my lap.

He cut me a glance, but my voice wouldn't work. He backed out of his chair, faced the cinder block right behind him, and ran his fingers down the concrete. "You have any idea what it's like to be closed in four walls every day?"

I toyed with my coat's zipper, lost for what to say.

He turned and looked at me head-on. No pretenses. Just straight, gut-wrenching vulnerability. "When you have no future, all you see is your past." He shook his head. "Worst part is it don't never change."

He returned to the table but didn't meet my eyes this time. He fidgeted with the corner of his jumper sleeve. "I know Dee would've—"

"Don't." I bolted up. My chair fell backward and clanked against the tile. Just hearing him say Dee's name ignited a flare inside me. "Don't act like you've changed. Like you care about Dee."

I wanted to launch the entire table at him, but all I could do was stand there with anger quivering down my body. "You think I don't know about you blackmailing our landlord?" Did he think I was stupid?

"What you talking about?"

Why did I ever think he'd be willing to undo the damage he'd caused? I yanked my chair up from the floor and shoved it against the table. "Don't bother with the act."

Trey set a hand over my trembling shoulder. "I think it's time to leave."

A guard had already reached Tito's side when I turned to face Trey. He stretched his arm across my shoulders and led me forward.

I peered behind me as Tito and the guard approached the door leading back to his cell. Another geyser of anger went off and whipped me around.

Trey held a hand in front of the guard escorting us out. "Give her a minute," he said with more authority than he had. The guard nodded to the one at the opposite end of the room, who stopped Tito at the door.

I marched straight up to him. No restraint. Nothing standing in the way of giving him a piece of my mind. Until I got close enough to see the piercing look of hopelessness in his eyes. It was a look I'd seen before. From Dee.

The moment closed in. Walls fell. And as a whisper rose inside me, all I could say was the one thing I hadn't planned. "I forgive you."

Confusion tore across Tito's face the same way it had over Dee's when he'd received an offer of grace instead of judgment.

Fragmented memories blurred into the scene in front

of me and gripped me between the two until the guard withdrew a set of keys. I blinked away the tear-stained memories but couldn't erase their impact. My eyes found Tito's. "I forgive you," I whispered again.

With our gazes fixed on each other, Tito and I both flinched at the sound of the heavy door unlocking. He stopped over the threshold and gaped back at me as the door closed between us.

I stayed still a minute longer, staring past walls of judgment into eyes of grace Dee had never let me forget. I'd clung to his plea to be courageous this whole time, but I never thought it would include forgiving Tito. Was that what he'd meant? Had he known all along?

I retraced my steps across the square tiles toward Trey's intuitive smile.

Dee had known I had to come here. So had Trey. And now, so did I.

Unlike when we arrived, I only halfway noticed the surroundings leading back to the car. Trey didn't say a word all the way home. He didn't need to.

His Honda idled beside the curb in front of my apartment. I opened the door but stopped, leaned across the seat, and gave him a hug. "Thanks."

He patted my back. "All I did was drive."

"And help me face things I couldn't see on my own." I shook my head at him. "Just an ordinary day with Trey Williams."

His laugh filled the entire car. "It's all about—"

"Perspective, I know." *Speaking of which.* I waved a

finger at him. "I think we should really put some para-meters around this whole perspective mantra thing."

Another throaty laugh. "You have it down more than you realize, kid." He tipped his head at my building. "Now, go on and get some rest."

Hard to argue with that. The afternoon had been more than a little draining.

I plodded out of the car and up the sidewalk. A hundred questions from the day had circled through my mind by the time I reached the door. I couldn't shake Tito's comment about the past never changing. But what if the future was just as unforgiving? While he might've been losing his future, I was losing my past—one I still wasn't ready to let go of.

I filed into the stairwell behind a girl who lived across the hall.

Riley lunged up from the steps, looking like he'd been holed up in a hospital waiting room. "Hey."

"Hey."

My floor mate squeezed around him and jogged up the stairs.

I angled my head. "You been waiting a while?"

He leaned against the railing and rubbed the back of his neck. "Just wanted to be here when you got home in case—"

"I was a blubbering mess?"

He laughed while dropping off the last step. "Better than a worried fiancé, kicking himself for not going with you."

Something about seeing him waiting for me, knowing I'd need him, set off another round of the day's already-wired emotions.

I stumbled into his chest and sank into the comfort his arms always provided.

Riley kissed the crown of my head. Rather than saying anything, he simply held me close and let me linger in the one place that silenced every other noise.

"Sorry. I think all that's been going on is catching up to me. Reminding me how easily time can be stolen from you." I nuzzled my face close to his neck. "I just don't want to take any of it for granted."

His grin brushed against my hair. "You're the last person who needs to worry about that."

I leaned back. He had to be joking.

His steadfast smile deepened. "The first time we passed each other on campus, you know what I saw in your eyes? Everything I'd almost given up on ever finding again." He rested his forehead to mine. "You don't take life for granted, Em. You live it with purpose."

Purpose. That was what I wanted more than anything. To make a lasting impact. Not to live in fear of what I could lose.

With my hand in his, I held on to the truths God never stopped teaching me. No matter what it cost, I'd sow all I had into what mattered most. Even when it meant confronting my deepest fears.

19

CREDENTIALS

THREE WEEKS of staying busy with classes and schoolwork would've been a nice distraction if the fast pace weren't driving the semester closer to deadlines I wasn't ready for.

Being less than a month away from our lease termination was bad enough without wondering what kind of backlash Nick had in store for Riley now that his intended February tour start date had passed. And I didn't even want to think about Jaycee and Trevor moving off-campus soon. All of it wrung my stomach in knots as we pulled up in front of the center.

Riley cut the engine. "Ready to take the spotlight, Miss Business Degree?"

I unbuckled my seat belt. "You had to go there, didn't you?" Like I wasn't nervous enough. Why had I agreed to this? "I'm not sure I'm even qualified to teach. Graduation isn't for another three months."

Riley tilted his head at me. "Having a piece of paper to mount on the wall isn't what makes you a good teacher."

I lifted my book bag from the floorboard and hugged it in my lap. "Yeah, well, experience might help."

"You kidding? You've been doing this for months. Just in a different context."

I leaned my head against the rest and stared at the tan headliner. Working with the kids one-on-one was entirely different from leading a class of adults.

A whiff of cinnamon and cloves lured my focus toward a cup of chai he was waving in front of me. I reached for it, eyes widening. After putting it in the cup holder to cool off, I'd gotten so lost in my thoughts, I'd forgotten about it. A slow smile tugged the corners of my mouth. I couldn't fight it. One taste of those sweet Indian spices, and I was ready to testify that the drink was some type of therapeutic tonic. My lashes fluttered.

His grin toppled into a laugh. "Guess all superheroes get their mojo from somewhere."

The tea almost sprayed through my nose. I gulped down my own laughter and wiped my chin with my sleeve. He always knew how to put me at ease. "Thanks."

Riley winked and stretched into the back seat. "One more reminder that you've got this." He set a gift bag on my lap.

My wary glance didn't faze his smile. I pulled out the tissue paper and froze. Jasmine's wooden music box stared up at me. I lifted the lid and traced my fingers over the word *Dream* stenciled inside.

Riley's thumb brushed over my cheek. "You have a song to share, remember?"

Memories from last year, when he'd loaned me the music box during a time I'd needed it most, climbed from my heart straight for my eyes and ended in a kiss that said everything I couldn't.

He lifted me back. "Think we better get inside," he said, voice raspy.

Good idea.

Almost across the street, my cell rang. I stopped on the sidewalk. "Hello?"

"Emma, this is Neal Chandler from the Success Foundation. I got your message."

So much for my chai's calming effects. "Yes?" I slanted into the bricks and held my breath. Riley's face contorted with question. I motioned for him to go in without me, but he flashed me a *yeah, right* expression.

"I'm calling to let you know I reopened your grant request," Mr. Chandler said.

The morning's muddled concerns sputtered out in an exhale. "That's… that's amazing. Thank you so much for your reconsideration. I promise it's a worthwhile cause."

"I have no doubt it is. Your proposal is quite impressive. I'm sorry it was overlooked."

Overlooked?

Riley angled his head. "What?" he mouthed.

I chewed the corner of my thumb, curious about Mr. Brake but afraid to stir up anything I didn't need to.

"Our committee will review your file, and I should have some more information for you in the next few weeks."

Now I had no choice but to ask. Deep breath. "Mr. Brake isn't on the committee, is he?"

Riley wove his fingers through mine, probably putting all the pieces together by now.

My heart had to have beat a hundred times, waiting for Mr. Chandler's delayed response.

"Jim's no longer with the Success Foundation." The statement lacked any intonation. Just straight, matter-of-fact business.

How much time had I wasted, not trying to reach them any sooner? "As of when?"

Another weighty pause. "This past week, actually." Mr. Chandler cleared his throat. "I have a meeting to run to, but I can assure you I'll be in touch as soon as I have an update."

"Of course. Thank you for calling. Talk to you soon." I hung up but didn't move until the conversation fully sank in. This could be the breakthrough we needed. A twinge of reservation warned me not to cling to hope, but the look in Riley's eyes reminded me there was nothing else worth holding on to.

"They reopened our proposal."

"Congratulations." He squeezed me to his side and led me down the walkway to the office.

My mind was still reeling when we walked in. Darius held open the back door for a few of the girls to pass through.

"Where's Trey?"

He glanced at the clock on the wall. "Said he had to run an errand. Left about ten minutes ago."

Which meant I'd have to wait to tell him about the grant possibility until after class. *Class.* Mr. Chandler's call had sidetracked me. I stared at the door to the classroom I'd gone in and out of too many times to count over the last nine months. It felt like a completely different place today.

On the other side of the doorway, my feet stopped at the edge of the packed classroom filled with people I didn't know.

Riley laced his fingers through mine again. Funny how much difference such a little thing could make. He kissed my cheek. "Just be yourself."

I still wasn't quite ready to let go of his hand. "Stay?"

"Already planned on it." He pointed behind him. "I'll be in the back."

And I'd be in the front—the last place I wanted to be.

Swallowing, I headed to my post and gripped the sides of a podium seated on top of a table. Riley reclined against the windowsill, blending into the sea of students, all of whom were probably waiting for me to remember I was the teacher.

I set my tea to the side and withdrew my notes from my book bag. The rustling of papers sounded twice as loud as it should have. After enough blinks to simulate a turbo fan, the words on the page came into focus.

"Miss Matthews?" Ms. Mendierez headed toward me from the front row. "I hope you don't mind. I told some of my friends about the class."

Some friends? More like the entire neighborhood.

A distinct line of dignity tightened across her forehead. "We're tired of things being the way they are." Her gaze briefly wandered behind her. "We might not be the most educated group, but we came 'cause we're ready for things to change."

Her conviction dismantled every bit of uneasiness I had. If they had the courage to learn, then I could find the courage to teach. I returned her smile as she made her way back to her seat.

I twisted my necklace. "Thank you all for coming. Welcome to Financial Planning. My name is Emma Matthews."

I smoothed out the ruffled corners of my papers and the tiny quiver left in my voice. "I don't pretend to be an expert on the subject, but I'd like to share some principles I hope will lay a solid foundation for you to build on. So, let's go ahead and get started." I set my finance textbook nearby. Just in case.

"How many of you have an IRA, either Simple or Roth?"

Instead of raised hands, a torrent of blank stares followed my question.

"How about an investment portfolio?"

Still, not a single hand lifted. Several people hung their heads and picked at scratches in their desks.

"A savings account?" I was grasping at straws. "Okay. Um…" I snatched up my textbook as my mind raced for a different starting point.

From the back of the room, Riley nodded and, somehow, I knew.

I let go of my text and, with it, the security I'd been afraid to release. It wasn't like me to abandon my notes, but Riley was right this morning. Even as informative as classroom instruction could be, sometimes everyday life experiences were the best teachers.

I veered out from behind the podium and sat on the front edge of the table. "Let's start with a more basic question. How many of you have a vision for what you'd like to do with your life?"

A few timid hands lifted in the air.

"Maybe it's the dream of starting your own business," I said. "Or maybe there's something you're good at—something you enjoy investing your time in—but you aren't quite sure how it could be a financial tool."

An older woman in the front row sat tall and tucked uncooperative strands of wiry gray hair back into her bun. "Ever since I was a little girl, I've wanted to open me a diner." Her eyes brimmed with flickers of a long-held dream. "I'd call it, Mama's Café."

"Mrs. Jackson makes the best hushpuppies in the city," a man a few rows back piped in.

The woman slumped in her seat and waved off his

comment. "But I don't know nothing about running no business."

"That's okay. Business can be learned." I walked along the first row. I knew that look of self-doubt. Was well acquainted with the power of insecurities. I squatted to her eye level. "Your courage to dream is your credential." My focus flittered toward Riley. "Someone just recently reminded me that a world of knowledge listed on a piece of paper doesn't amount to much without heart and character."

Her smile almost outshined his. Nothing like having your own life lessons hit you square in the chest.

I returned to the front table. "I can teach you practical steps on how to manage finances, but never lose sight of where it all begins." I scanned the room. "Stepping out in faith is what'll make the difference between wishing things were different and seeing them change."

My heart was about to break through my rib cage. The words flowed with such confidence, it felt like someone else was talking through me—as if I were merely a part of the audience.

I called Riley up and asked him to tell his own story of daring to believe in his dream of becoming a recording artist. One by one, we went around the classroom and each shared a tucked-away aspiration. For some, it was the first time acknowledging it publicly. For a few, it was the first time even identifying it to themselves.

Even though each goal was attainable, a crisis of

confidence tainted almost everyone the same way it had for Dee the day he first showed me his drawings.

A lack of talent or ability didn't hold them back. A lack of hope did. We'd be kidding ourselves if we expected that to change overnight. It'd take perseverance, along with the one thing we were running out of.

I didn't think my heart could break over the center closing any more than it already had. But seeing Ms. Mendierez's face light up from the front row as she mouthed "thank you," left me completely undone.

How could we start this class without being able to finish? Would the little time we had together be enough? I hedged back the thought and ended the class before the lump trekking up my throat became audible.

Chairs screeched backward. Conversations picked up. And I simply stood there, searching for answers I didn't have.

The group of students gradually dissolved until the last stragglers exited, leaving Riley and me alone. He sauntered up beside me. "My brave fiancée."

"I'm not sure stumbling my way through a class counts as—"

A yell from outside pummeled through the walls.

Riley and I exchanged one glance and launched out the door.

A woman's angry sobs caught me short before we rounded the bend. I'd seen too much loss mar that street corner to handle any more. I inched around with Riley by my side.

Trey and a woman from the class held Ms. Mendierez up by the arms in front of some kind of oversized poster tacked onto the building. Beneath it, someone had strewn layers of garbage and debris across the sidewalk around a chalk outline of a body.

I edged close enough to risk getting a look at the wall. Vivid memories from the night Dee died rebounded off the poster into my gut—the stench of must and blood, the sirens against the whispers. The same loss of balance gripped me now.

Someone had blown up a grainy picture of Dee's broken body in my arms on the street, blood seeping through his clothes. Dark, bold text topped the image: *CLOSE THE CENTER BEFORE YOU END UP LIKE THIS.*

How could anyone's callousness stretch this far?

Ms. Mendierez broke free and crumbled to the sidewalk. "Who'd do this?"

After visiting Tito, I honestly wasn't sure anymore. But that didn't stop tremors of fury from coursing through me. I'd go to the city. Talk to whomever I needed to. Someone had to stop this.

"Mr. Williams?"

We all turned toward our landlord as he approached. He swiped off his hat and took in the scene, looking all around as if scouting for the nearest escape route.

Trey met him on the sidewalk. "Mr. Glyndon, what are you doing here?"

He fiddled with his hat. "I got an email. Said to meet you here at three."

"An email from who?"

"I assumed it was you." The skin around the bridge of Mr. Glyndon's nose wrinkled. He backed up. "I shouldn't be here."

Trey reached for him. "Wait—"

A news van zipped up to the curb right in front of us. A microphone and camera were in our faces before we had time to blink. "Mr. Glyndon, can you tell us what's going on here?" a woman with entirely too much makeup on asked.

Sweat beaded across his red forehead. "I... I don't understand. How did you know...? I shouldn't..."

Someone must have tipped them off.

Miss Ruby Lips flung the microphone back. "Is it true this is your rental property? What do you have to say about the statement someone's trying to make today?" She motioned for the cameraman to sweep a wide shot across the wall and sidewalk where Ms. Mendierez still sat on her knees.

Mr. Glyndon's gaze flitted in every direction and landed past the camera. His face paled. Clutching his hat, he backed up again. I traced his line of sight and caught a sliver of that same BMW pulling away.

I turned in front of Mr. Glyndon and blocked the camera with my back. "Please. This needs to end. Whatever someone's got on you isn't worth what it's costing these families."

A stream of sweat coursed down his cheek. He blinked away from me toward Trey. "I'm sorry. I... I can't."

The reporter butted her microphone in between us. If he wouldn't man up, I would. I turned and pointed to the scene. "The only statement this person made is that he's nothing more than a common thug who resorts to vandalism and threats to get his way. But we're not going anywhere."

A couple of our younger kids, who'd apparently been eavesdropping, slinked around the corner and raced right into Trey's and my legs. I picked up Teneecia. She swirled a red Blow Pop in her mouth. After one peek at the camera, she turned and flung her arms around me.

"This isn't just a rental property." I stroked her hair. "It's a second home for kids who are counting on us to keep it open. We're in the process of raising the necessary funds as we speak. We're even planning a service day next week. Something the kids can be involved in."

I resituated Teneecia on my hip. "By helping out, they'll be gaining a real sense of responsibility and investment—things we're teaching them every day in our programs. Not to mention the chance to experience how they can use their own resources to make a difference." I darted a pointed glance at Mr. Glyndon. "We could all use a little more of that."

The lights from the camera glared over his glistening forehead. "And Mr. Glyndon, what's your take on this organization? Will you be supporting it?"

A series of swallows passed. "Yes. Of course." Backing him into a corner in front of the media seemed to have oiled up his jaw with the one thing he always caved under. Pressure. "We were discussing the extension on rent before you arrived."

Sure we were. At this point, I'd let him worry about detangling himself from his growing web of lies. Between the money we could raise from the service day and the second chance the Success Foundation was giving us, hopefully we'd have him out of our hair for a solid year.

I shrank out of the spotlight while he floundered for a way out of his own. The reporters could have him.

Teneecia coasted off my hip, and I helped Ms. Mendierez up from the ground. We tore down the poster, crumbled the intended harm into a tight wad that belonged with the rest of the trash at our feet, and stood our ground on the one thing we were all learning to fight for. Hope.

20

RECONSTRUCTION

A WEEK and a half wasn't long enough to mend the sting that poster had left but focusing on our service event was a huge help in pressing forward.

Darius towered above me, scraping paint off the basketball pole with a little too much enthusiasm. I flicked a paint chip off my cheek for the hundredth time that morning. "How about we switch places again?"

Teetering on my toes, I made a valiant attempt to transition from squatting to standing without falling on my face. Darius's laughter followed him all the way to the ground.

"Hey, you try standing up after sitting like that for an hour, and we'll see who's still laughing."

"'Cept I ain't old." He did a series of squats like he was a professional weightlifter.

I chiseled away, making sure at least half of my chips conveniently fell spot on his head.

At least he provided entertainment. With all the hard work we'd been putting in, I couldn't argue needing a laugh. It was more than worth it though. The turnout for our service day had already exceeded my expectations.

All that publicity last week might've had something to do with it. That and the multi-colored flyers Trey had practically wallpapered the city in. Though, I had a feeling the edgy competition between break dancing and spoken word contests happening out front was the real driving source of attention at the moment.

People funneled back to the string of tables we'd set up, each with pairs of kids seated behind them ready to share their talents. Handmade bracelets. Hair braiding stations. Artwork displays.

It was probably the first time they ever saw how their skills could serve a greater purpose. Despite how much money we raised for the center today, watching the kids gain a sense of self-worth made the entire event worthwhile.

Even the weather cooperated. I held my chisel between my knees, stripped off my sweatshirt, and tied it around my waist. A refreshing breeze swam over my bare arms in a gentle nudge to keep working. I stretched my neck from side to side and lifted on my tiptoes to continue scraping the pole.

A commotion broke out behind me. Turning, I squinted under the sunlight and dropped my chisel to the ground.

"Mr. A. J.," one of the girls called. "You're back!"

With a gallon of paint in his hand, A. J. stopped when his eyes met mine. He diverted his attention to the horde of excited kids practically mosh-pitting him. "Missed you guys too."

Hugs and pant leg climbing ensued. Until little Andre approached. The crowd parted and left them standing face to face in a silent duel. It was hard to blame Andre for his cautious stare. It had killed him when A. J. didn't come back.

A. J. crouched to the six-year-old's eye level and held out his hand in a peace offering.

Andre's stone-like expression didn't break. He flung both fists onto his hips above evenly spaced-out legs. "Not so fast," he said with an impressive county sheriff accent.

I covered my mouth to shield my laughter.

His hands trailed down his sides, his stoicism cracking. "You ditched us, Mr. A. J."

A. J.'s shoulders drooped. The collision of vulnerability and remorse on his face was enough to back my already-weary legs against the pole behind me.

He swallowed, inhaled, and slowly raised his head to meet the gut-wrenching look in Andre's eyes. "I'm sorry. I... had some things I had to work through." His gaze drifted from Andre to me with a level of transparency I doubted even a six-year-old would miss. "But I'm ready to come back now. If you'll have me."

Andre exchanged a hesitant glance with his buddy, standing beside him. Thirty seconds of indecision led to an extended hand topped with a smile I hadn't seen in months. They shared their famous handshake, but Andre held on a minute longer. "Just promise not to bounce again, a'ight?"

A. J. tried to keep a straight face. "A'ight."

Andre leaned over to his friend as they strutted away. "Girls," he whispered. "They make us do crazy things sometimes."

If there'd been any question that Andre deserved the world's most adorable kid ever award, he just obliterated it.

Pardoned of his crimes, A. J. rose to his feet and headed over. "Heard you guys could use some help today." He held up the bucket of paint and offered his usual disarming smile.

I snagged my chisel from the ground and turned it 'round and 'round in my hands. "Well, I suppose if our local sheriff let you off the hook, then I guess we can accept your help."

"How very gracious of you." Still a few feet away, he kept his eyes on me, seemingly unaware of anyone else around.

Silence hovered.

It didn't feel like he was searching for the right words. More like they weren't necessary. At least, not to him.

Darius stretched up from the ground with perfect ease. *Figures.*

He clasped A. J.'s hand. "What up, bro? Welcome home."

"Thanks, man. You been running the court while I've been gone?"

Darius wedged the chisel under his waistband, kicked a basketball up from the ground, and dribbled it between his legs. "You know it."

A. J. swiped the ball from him and nailed a backhand layup. "Good thing I'm back to show you up."

"Psh. You wish, dawg." Darius followed up his remark with an effortless three-pointer.

Boys.

The basketball thudded against the pavement and rolled off to the side near the grill where Mr. Jenkins was killing me with those amazing barbecue scents.

"Ohhh." Shouts and hollers echoed from the competition still brewing up front, drawing Darius's glance.

A. J.'s stare bounced from the street back to him. "Why don't you let me take over here? I think those playas are waiting for you to show off your mad popping skills."

Darius busted out his crazy dance moves while handing over his chisel. He shuffled backward until he reached the fence, then sprinted toward the front of the building.

A. J. flipped the chisel in the air as he edged near with his attention fastened on me again. I backed up and bumped into the pole. His dimples caved into his cheeks with whatever he wasn't saying.

I straightened out my shirt. "What?"

He pointed to the side of my face. "You have a bit of paint…"

I swiped my hand across my cheek without thinking. Great, I'd probably just made it worse.

Laughing, he steadied his hand over top of mine and lowered it to my side. "Here. Let me get it." He rubbed the tip of his thumb across my skin.

I looked away. "A. J., I…"

He stepped back and brandished his chisel. "Guess I'll start at the top." Towering above me, he began scraping the sections I'd never be able to reach.

The pavement met my knees in a welcome reprieve from standing under the weight of his smile.

How were we supposed to do this? Work side by side after everything? The kids needed him here. Trey needed the help. I couldn't be the reason he stayed away. But I couldn't see how we were supposed to make this work.

"So," I said after another quiet minute. "You're back for good?"

The shrill sound of metal against metal stopped. "This is where I belong." Without taking his eyes off the pole, he laughed sadly. "Being defiant doesn't always turn out so well." The scraping resumed and almost drowned out his soft voice. "Even when we're convinced we know a better way."

I stared at the ground, hating the hint of heartache in his words.

His hand grazed the edge of my chin. "Hey, it's fine."

Is that what he called it?

"I'll make you a deal."

Oh boy. This couldn't be good.

His ambiguous grin only made it worse. "I'll work out my schedule with Trey so I'm here only on days when you're not, if…"

I sat back on my heels. "If?"

"If," he said, still grinning, "you let me pick out the song for our dance at Trevor and Jaycee's wedding."

That was my end of the bargain? "Um, sorry to burst your bubble, but that's kind of a lost cause. Trust me. There isn't a single detail of Jae's wedding that she hasn't had planned since she was sixteen."

"I don't know. I can be pretty convincing."

I rolled my eyes. "Good luck with that. Not even your best man status will score you enough points on this one."

Unabashed confidence flashed across A. J.'s face.

Perfect. Just what he needed. A challenge.

He reached for the half-chiseled section of paint above him. "We'll see."

I didn't have to see. I *knew*. "Don't say I didn't warn you." I laughed until what he'd said earlier sank in. I'd been so distracted by the second part of his proposition that I'd overlooked the first. He said he'd come back to the center only on days when I wasn't there.

I stared past the court into a blur of thoughts. He was keeping his word. That day in the gym, he promised to respect my choice to disconnect our heart tie.

A. J.'s whistle drew me back to the moment. "If you scrape that section any longer, you're going to cut straight through it."

The scratched-up pole blinked into view. "Sorry. Just thinking."

A series of car honks rang up front, followed by a roar of whoops and hollers. I shared a hesitant glance with A. J., dropped my chisel, and sprang toward the source of all the commotion.

A tour bus with the words *Biggie Rey* running down the middle took up most of the street in front of our building. The kids who'd been dancing earlier all congregated around it like roadies waiting for some star to emerge through the door.

Andre strutted over to us with his arms crossed. He might've been able to pull off the tough look if his smile weren't glowing. "Mr. A. J., you have somethin' to do with this?"

"Sorry, bro. Wish I were that cool."

I looked between them. "Someone want to fill me in, here?"

Andre's already-widened eyes nearly doubled in size. He tapped A. J.'s leg. "She's just playin' us, right?"

A. J. kept his mouth shut. *Smart man.*

I knelt to Andre's side, waiting to be schooled.

He pointed at the bus. "Biggie Rey."

"And he is...?"

Andre shifted his weight to one leg, cocked his head,

and stared at me like I'd been locked in a bomb shelter for the length of his life.

Darius strolled up beside us. "Dang, girl, where you been living? He's only, like, the flyest rapper on the music scene right now."

I pressed on my thighs to stand up. "Sorry. Never heard of him."

A laugh met me a foot away. "I'll try not to take that personally." A hefty guy about my age, surrounded by a swarm of kids failing miserably at playing it cool, stood in front of me. He extended a hand. "Rey Alvarez. You must be Emma."

I shook his hand on autopilot while looking at A. J. for some clue on how this was happening.

He pointed behind him. "Yo, is it a'ight if we park here for now? It'll take us about an hour to set up."

Andre squeezed himself between us. "Setting up? You mean, like a concert? You's playin' right here? Stop messin' with me."

Rey laughed. "I'm not messin'. I even got a few back-stage passes."

Andre busted out a Michael Jackson spin. I caught him by the shoulders and eyed the big-time rapper who'd somehow landed in front of our building. "I'm sorry. I'm afraid I must be missing something."

"Riley didn't tell you about the benefit concert? Wow, my boy's one smooth dawg, keeping it a surprise. I gotta give him props next time I see him."

Riley. Music scene. Benefit concert. The pieces

threaded together a fragment at a time. "He put you up to this?"

"Said you guys could use some help raising funds." Rey flicked his chin toward the building. "I grew up in a place like this in Philly." He took off his cap and fit it over Andre's head. "We do what we can. Right, little dawg?"

Andre ran his fingers over the bill of the hat, too enthralled to answer.

I fought back an unsolicited rise of emotion. "Thank you. I don't know what to say."

"You don't gotta say nothin'." He motioned for his crew. "We'll take care of everything." Halfway to the back, he turned. "But you do gots to promise me you'll stay for the show so you can say you've heard of Biggie Rey now." Laughing, he spun around and disappeared onto the court—away from my burning cheeks.

A. J. leaned a shoulder into mine. "That was pretty cool of Riley."

"The keeping it a secret part?" Which he was definitely gonna hear about.

"That, too, now that you mention it." His dimples sank beneath his cheekbones. "Just think. Now you can ask Biggie Rey for some dancing tips."

He had to remind me of the wedding dance, didn't he? One of the crew members shuffled by, carrying a drum. A. J. was lucky I didn't shove his head straight into it.

"It's not funny. You've seen me try to dance."

"It's choreographed. I'm sure it'll be fine."

Choreographed or not, I still had to dance in front of hundreds of people. "If an absolute nightmare waiting to happen qualifies as fine, then, yeah, you're right."

There were those stinking dimples again. "Relax, Rosy. You've got a killer dance partner."

That was what worried me the most.

A. J. caught the corner of a speaker about to fall off a dolly and jumped right in, helping to bring the rest of the equipment to the back.

Rubbing my arms, I stared at the bus—half-flustered that Riley hadn't told me about it, half-overwhelmed by the ways he loved me, but mostly moved that we weren't fighting this battle alone. The center was going to be okay.

My favorite sideways smile appeared around the bus's front bumper.

"You." I scrunched my lips and squinted.

"Sorry, can't help myself. That adorable look is worth it every time." Riley hopped over the curb and met me on the sidewalk.

I shoved him in the arm.

He stumbled backward, still laughing. "You're not really mad, are you?"

Madly in love with him. I hooked a finger through his belt loop and drew him close. "I can't believe you thought to do this. Thank you."

"I'm not the only one whose dreams matter." He lifted my chin. "We're in this together, right?"

Dolly wheels squeaked behind us. A guy from Biggie Rey's crew headed back to the bus for more equipment. The sight of A. J. tailing him reignited my earlier apprehension about Jaycee's wedding party plans.

I kept my eyes on Riley. He was right. We were in this together. All of it. *Please let him remember that when I have to dance with A. J.*

21

DANCE OFF

"SORRY," I said after stepping on A. J.'s foot for the umpteenth time.

Jaycee knew heels and I rarely made a good combination. Add dance moves into the mix, and it was a recipe for disaster. Especially when my mind was still reeling from the benefit concert. The awareness it'd stirred for the center would've been enough all by itself, but to have raised five thousand dollars in only a couple of hours? I couldn't wrap my head around it.

A pair of shimmery Palazzo pants flittered by us as our dance instructor followed Jaycee's signal to pause the MP3 player. "Okay, everyone. Let's start from the top. *Again.*"

"Jae, I told you this was a bad idea." I pulled my hair tie loose, flipped my head over, and doubled the band around another attempt at a ponytail. "If we can just practice without heels, I might be able to—"

"You're going to be dancing in heels." She marched straight up to us. "You might as well practice in them."

"Now, now, ladies." A. J. patted us both on the back. "We don't need any cat fights tonight."

Jaycee and I shared a glance long enough to wink in agreement and both turned at the same time to punch A. J. in the shoulders. He didn't so much as stumble backward. Stupid muscles. He laughed his way across the floor to Trevor.

I dawdled in front of Jaycee, flexing my ankles back and forth to the ground. It didn't matter if I hated heels. This was important to her. "Sorry."

"Me too."

A. J. reemerged by my side. "Don't worry, Jae. I'm on it." He stood tall with his feet together like a soldier reporting for duty. "Nothing a few private dance lessons can't cure."

I rolled my eyes. "Not gonna happen, buddy."

His stubborn smile begged to differ.

Our dance instructor clapped her hands. "Places, everyone." If her mousy voice weren't comical enough, her sweatbands topped it off.

She cued the music from the top. A. J. opened his frame in an invitation to join him. "Shall we?"

I grudgingly took his hand.

He leaned forward. "Try to relax. Let me do the leading."

The instructor walked by right as I opened my mouth

to offer some grandiose rebuttal. "Back straight, shoulders down." She lifted my chin. "Head up. That's it."

I held the pose until she passed. It took everything in me not to smack the grin off A. J.'s face. "You're really enjoying this, aren't you?"

"You have no idea." His smile stretched so far I wasn't sure how he managed to make his jaw work.

It was like reliving our basketball game all over again. Man, I hated letting him win.

The instructor glided across the dance hall, weaving around the evenly spaced-out couples. "Now, feel the beat of the music. Let it guide your steps. And don't forget to count. One, two, three. One, two, three."

Her sentences flowed like melodic chants. Seriously, how many yoga classes had this chick sat in on? I feigned a compliant smile as she floated past us again.

A. J. rested my hand over his chest. "C'mon, Em. Let the beat guide your steps." He tapped his finger over mine. "*Gu-gung, gu-gung.*"

"And who are you supposed to be? Patrick Swayze?"

He busted out laughing.

Ms. Jane Fonda Lookalike whipped a troubled glare in our direction and cleared her throat.

A. J. straightened and drew me into position again. "Hey," he whispered, "don't make me break out my real dance moves. The kids were giving me lessons on Saturday. I got skills that'll make you dizzy."

"Ahem. No talking on the dance floor, please. Stay in

step. One, two, three," she practically hummed. "Yes, that's it. Very good."

Her ethereal pants flowed behind her as she glided past us.

Hmm, a yoga dance instructor fairy. A. J. was lucky she didn't have a wand I could steal from her.

As soon as she faded from view, I smirked at him. "You wish you had moves like that. If I weren't in these heels, you'd be the dizzy one."

Did he just snort?

He dished out another haughty smile. "Let's not forget the last time you tried to beat me. I seem to remember that being somewhat of an..." He twirled me across the floor and drew me back in until I almost bumped him in the face. "...*Embarrassing* moment for you."

What I would've given to throw a basketball at his gut right then. I pitched my nose in the air and looked away from him. "You had an unfair advantage."

He drew me even closer. "You mean, like now?"

Ms. Fairy Queen floated by us on another celestial sweep around the room. "Lovely hold. Very nice."

The couple to our right obscured her behind them. I stomped on A. J.'s foot while I had the chance. "Sorry." I wrenched my shoulders in the air. "Slipped."

The music slowed to an instrumental close. I curtseyed and returned the same impish smile following A. J.'s bow.

He applauded my successful completion of the dance

and leaned forward. "See? You *can* do it. All you need is a little distraction."

I opened my mouth, but nothing came out. He'd egged me on because he knew it'd keep my mind off the moves. After everything, he was still rescuing me when I needed it.

He spun past me on his way toward the bag he'd thrown in the corner of the room when he'd first arrived. Instead of stopping in the bathroom to change, he tossed the bag over his shoulder and headed for the exit. "It's been fun," he said, "but I need to get going. I have a date I can't miss."

"A date?"

He wheeled around, chuckling with something resembling flattery. "Don't sound so surprised, Rosy."

"I'm not." In fact, I was relieved. Happy he'd moved on. That was all I'd ever wanted for him—happiness.

He reached behind him for the door handle. "I'm taking Andre to a basketball game tonight. Peace offering." With a wink to match his maddening grin, he disappeared through the door.

A breeze snuck a pair of furled maple leaves inside before the door closed. The cool air blew through my hair and fanned the instructor's pants as she sailed over to bring Jaycee her MP3 player.

She stopped between us, followed my gaze to the back of the door, and placed her delicate hand on my forearm. "You two make a lovely dance couple. But if I may offer a little piece of advice." She leaned in close enough to whisper, as if trying to spare me from embarrassment. "Don't be afraid to let him lead."

I couldn't help it. I laughed until no sound came out and the lady's bewildered expression forced me to bite my tongue.

Jaycee grabbed my arm and steered me in the opposite direction. "Sorry," she said to the instructor. "The stress is starting to make us all a little delirious."

I'd regained my composure by the time we made it to the opposite wall. "Sorry, Jae. Her comment... the irony..."

"Uh-huh," Jaycee mumbled through a tight-lipped smile. "I think it's about time you lose those heels. They're starting to affect your mind." She tossed me a water bottle and my purse. "C'mon. Let's get out of here. Starbucks is calling."

NOTHING LIKE A VENTI chai tonic to put things back in perspective. Jaycee and I were still laughing as we strode up the sidewalk to our apartment, arm in arm. If nothing else, the dance would most certainly end up being entertaining.

Jake met us midway to the door and rubbed his snout under my hand as Riley rose from the porch. "How'd it go?"

I looked down at my sore feet. "You mean before or

after we had to restart the dance for the hundredth time?"

"She was great. Don't let her fool you." Jaycee slanted me a pointed look. "Just a little stubborn."

Riley strolled toward us. "You don't say?"

I shook my head at both of them. "Ha. Ha."

Expression sobering, he squatted and rustled Jake's ears. Was he thinking about me dancing with A. J.?

Jaycee looked from Riley to me and jutted her coffee cup toward the door. "I'm going to go get out of these clothes. Think I might hit the gym for a bit." She breezed past Riley and jogged up to the door with a level of energy that should've been zapped after that dance lesson.

The gym? Seriously? Maybe I needed to give the whole coffee buzz thing a try.

Riley stood and tucked his hands in his pockets. Jake lay down beside him and rested his chin over his paws. "Hope you don't mind me waiting for you."

"Of course not. But first things first." I grabbed his arm for balance and stripped off one shoe at a time. "This dance might not be a total disaster if I can manage to stay on my feet."

He smiled. "Trust me. No one's going to be looking at your feet."

I waved off his compliment. "You haven't even seen my dress yet."

"I wasn't talking about your dress."

Good thing the concrete was freezing. With any luck,

the cold seeping into the soles of my feet would drain the heat crawling up my neck. We'd probably never reach a point where he'd stop making me blush.

Riley laughed at my expression. "You still have no idea how easily you capture people's hearts, do you?"

"I'm pretty sure Jaycee will be the one to steal the show on her own wedding day."

"Not for me," he said without so much as a pause. "Though, seeing her in white might just make me wonder if I'm ever gonna get you in a wedding dress."

"Is that right?"

He inched closer. "Mm-hmm."

"Mr. Calm and Collected isn't getting anxious, is he?"

He feigned a look of innocence. "Me? No. I mean, if you don't count the times when I see you." He traced his hand down my arm to my fingers. "Or when I hear your voice," he said while linking both my arms around his back. "Or when I'm close enough to feel your heartbeat." He shrugged. "Other than that, I'm completely fine."

"Mm, yes, well, that does pose a problem, doesn't it?"

"The question is, what should we do about it?"

I scrunched my lips to the side. "We could ditch every reason we have for waiting and fly to Vegas right now."

He tossed his head back. "You're really trying to test the limits of my perseverance, aren't you?"

Like he didn't test mine every single time he looked at me.

His cell rang. He barely tipped it out of his pocket before dismissing the call.

It killed me to watch him ignore calls that were probably far more important than he let on. "Any update on rescheduling the tour?"

"Brett's working on it," he said like it was a passing comment about the weather instead of his career.

I backed up. "Riley, please—"

"You know what I've been thinking? Why not daydream?"

"Sorry?"

His fingertips found mine again. "Instead of worrying about all the question marks, why not view them as a chance to dream about the future?" He motioned toward the sky. "Kinda like cloud chasing."

His eyes brought me back to the first day we spent on the sports field when I'd told him how I used to drag Dad outside to see the shapes in the clouds. From the beginning, he'd made it so easy to open up to him. He'd gotten even better at being able to side-track me.

Riley expanded his smile until I returned it. "C'mon, top choice for a honeymoon?"

"Alaska."

"That was a quick answer."

"Always wanted to go. All that wide-open space. Pristine landscape." I shrugged. "My love of the outdoors, I guess."

He studied me. "A girl after my own heart. Top place to live?"

"Isn't that a given?"

His forehead pinched, gaze dropping. "We don't have to move to Nashville. The center…"

I couldn't blame him for not finishing. My own voice faltered at the thought.

Jake's collar jingled as he snapped his head toward a squirrel scurrying across the street. I knelt to rub his ears, grateful for the interruption. He rolled onto his back and arched his belly for me to pet instead.

"Saying goodbye won't be easy, but my life's with you." I stared absently at the pavement. As much as I wanted to start that life, I wasn't ready to think about the one I'd be leaving behind.

I pushed off the ground, dragged my hand around Riley's waistline as I passed, and moseyed up the walkway. Jake lumbered up and trotted after me. "What if we daydream about the wedding part instead?"

"We can start with our vows. You want to write them together?"

Shoulders lifted, I teetered on the balls of my feet. "Actually, I want to be surprised."

His face went blank. "Sure you didn't trade places with my fiancée on the way over?"

"What?" I splayed my hands to my sides.

Riley bent down to pick up my heels and met me at the stoop. "I'm a little shocked is all." He brushed back a strand of hair that'd blown horizontally in the wind. "You—the girl who bruised my arm over the whole Biggie Rey surprise?"

"Oh, stop. I didn't bruise you. And this is different.

We can coordinate some, but I want to hear you say them for the first time when we're standing at the altar. It means more to me that way. I can't explain it."

He brandished our favorite lawyer-look. "So, does that mean I can throw in some other surprises, and you won't be upset?"

I flaunted the look right back. "Maybe."

He laughed. "Now, there's the girl I know."

"What do you mean by surprise exactly?"

He folded his arms and left my heels dangling from his hand. "That kind of defeats the purpose of it being a surprise, doesn't it?"

"You're impossible sometimes, you know that?"

"And you're still adorable when you're flustered."

I strained to keep from mirroring his smile. Right. Caving, I turned and sat on the porch. "I got an email from Melody today."

"Really?" He joined me on the stoop, set my shoes to the side, and rubbed Jake's head.

I hugged my knees to my chest and raised my feet off the cold concrete. "She already has several songs picked out for us."

"I bet."

"Actually," I said, "they're pretty good. She's a natural at this sort of thing."

"I don't doubt it. My whole family lives and breathes music."

"You say that like it's a bad thing."

"It can be." He stared out in front of us.

A fragment of the mark where the wolf had bitten his arm poked out from behind his cuff. I pushed up his sleeve.

"It'll probably leave a scar," he said.

It couldn't be worse than the one his dad's words had left—even if it wasn't visible.

I tugged his sleeve back down and laced my fingers through his. "You know, I still want to wait for your dad's blessing on the wedding. It's important for him to be there... voluntarily." I leaned into his shoulder. "I'm not giving up hope."

"That's why I love you." He kissed my temple. "But honestly, Em, we can't wait forever."

"I know." Exhaling, I searched for a way to hold on and let go at the same time. "After graduation." I faced him. "Regardless of what else happens, let's set the date for June." Jaycee would be itching to plan another ceremony by then. Austin should be able to walk again. And that'd still leave enough time for his dad to come around, wouldn't it?

"Deal." Riley held out my shoes. "But how about we tackle one wedding at a time?"

I reluctantly took my heels back and sighed. "Deal."

22

TIME

My phone rang as I left my operations management class. Hands full, I swung my backpack around and squatted to the floor. Good thing the wall was there. I caught my balance and massaged my hamstring while fishing for my cell. After five dance rehearsals over the last two weeks, my muscles should've been used to stretching.

I clamped my phone to my ear with my shoulder, shoved my midterm review notes in my book bag, and zipped it up. "Hello."

"Your brother turns gimp, and you decide not to call him anymore?" Austin said with a healthy dose of his usual sarcasm.

I pushed up on my knees. "Sorry. It's been kinda crazy around here. I'm barely keeping my head on straight."

206 | CRYSTAL WALTON

"You're not killing yourself over this grant thing, are you?"

Nothing like a big brother's overprotective instincts kicking in.

"Just waiting." And praying. "We're doing what we can in the meantime." I backed open the door and squinted at the glare rippling off the sidewalk. Hard to believe we'd made it to March already. "The kids raised close to seven hundred dollars through this service project we did. And we got something like five K from a benefit concert."

I skidded beside one of the stone benches along the walkway. "Oh my word, Aust. I can't believe I forgot to tell you. The sales from Dee's drawings. Ms. Mendierez said they totaled almost two thousand dollars."

"I'm not surprised. My boy Rob said they'd probably go for a decent price."

That was for sure.

A breeze coursed up the walkway and found every tiny hole in my sweater. I resituated my backpack and kept trekking across the campus. "Thanks again for making that connection. It was a huge help. You should see the renovations we're doing to the basketball court. The kids are stoked. Actually, the adults, too. Seeing the kind of stuff that's possible has got this whole dreamer-buzz-thing stirring around that place. I don't know how to describe it."

Austin laughed.

Gimp or not, he was definitely getting a good pillow swat the next time I saw him. "I'm serious."

"I know. It's just funny how dead-on Dad was sometimes."

"What are you talking about?" I stopped along the bridge and folded my arms over the railing.

"He told me you'd end up running your own organization one day."

Really? "I'm only helping out—"

"You're leading more than you realize," he said with Dad's perfect intonation.

The creek ran downstream, lapping over the rocks the same way memories of Dad collected around my heart. "He always saw a world of dreams, didn't he?"

"He just saw what we couldn't."

And loaned his faith to us until we could.

"Matthews, you ready to roll?" someone in the background called.

"One sec," Austin answered. "Em, let me go. I gotta get some P. T. in if I'm gonna be ready in time for your wedding."

Even though Riley and I had finally set a date, something still felt unsettled, but I didn't want to get into that right now. "Love ya, Aust."

"You too. Later."

Another damp breeze swam off the gorge and spurred me the rest of the way to my apartment.

Inside, I hunched against the back of the door as I'd

done a thousand times over the last year and a half. Jaycee sat curled up in her usual corner of the couch, surrounded by a bundle of books. It all should've filed right in with countless other moments but thinking about Dad reminded me of how easily those moments slipped away.

Jaycee tapped the end of a gnawed-off pencil on her notepad without peeking up to say hi.

I kicked off my shoes and flopped onto the chair across from the couch. Still, not even a glance my way. "Everything all right?"

She dropped her pencil and glared at me.

Maybe I should've accepted the silence instead of interrupting it.

"All right?" She was up and pacing before I had time to haul my feet into the chair and out of her path. "If you equate all right with keeping my head on by a thread of sanity, then, yeah, I'm super." She snatched a sheet from a laundry basket of clean clothes on the coffee table. "They should really teach a class here on how to fold a fitted sheet. Practical. Isn't that what an education is supposed to be?"

I couldn't help it. Laughing was probably the most inappropriate response, but seeing her this frazzled made it impossible to hold it in.

Her expression contorted from stunned to offended to amused in the short time it took her to hurl the balled-up sheet at me.

She fell back onto the couch, laughing now too. "Sorry. I'm losing my mind. I mean, I love student teaching, and I'm not at all second-guessing wanting to be a teacher. It's just that the timing couldn't be worse with all the wedding planning I'm doing right now." She buried her face in a throw pillow. "I feel like my thoughts are running in a hundred different directions."

"Welcome to my perpetual state of existence." I scooted to the edge of the chair. "I'm sure it's nothing a girls' night out and Starbucks can't remedy."

Above the top of the pillow, Jaycee's eyes widened like a kid who'd been handed the world's largest ice cream cone but then shrank when she looked back at the pile of books on the couch. "I'll have to take a rain check. But you have no idea how much I could use Starbucks right now."

"I might have a slight idea," I said more to myself. I shoved my own jumbled thoughts aside, knowing she needed her best friend even more than coffee. I sat beside her and removed the books and papers from the space between us, never so glad she didn't have the additional pressure of planning my wedding right now as well.

She rested her head on my shoulder.

"I know moving up the date has kicked your stress level into high gear. But if anyone's organized enough to pull it off, it's you."

"Thanks." Jaycee lifted her head and drew the pillow in her lap even tighter. "Everything's actually coming together pretty smoothly. My mom's been a huge help. I think it's been a good distraction for her."

"See, you have a lot of people ready to help make this day perfect for you. Don't worry."

Jaycee towed one leg onto the couch and dragged the eraser side of the pencil in a sporadic pattern along her calf. "There's more to be nervous about than the ceremony."

We hadn't talked much about the honeymoon. I stumbled over a few words that weren't anywhere close to forming a sentence.

Jaycee cracked up. "You wait. Your turn's coming."

June wasn't that far away. I should've felt her same giddy nerves, not apprehension. I stole the pillow from her and bundled it under my arms. "You know, I was full-on ready to get married that night I went to Nashville. Then Riley came back, ready to elope too. But stuff with his contract and with A. J. and me... I don't know. I started worrying he was rushing it. And after meeting his family, I knew for sure we had to push it back to give him time to sort things out with his dad first. Then Austin had to go and break his leg and make me promise to wait until he can walk me down the aisle."

Clasping the top of my hair, I finally took a breath and looked at her. "You think that's all a bad sign? Like maybe someone's trying to tell us we're not ready?"

Jaycee shook her head. "What am I going to do when I don't get to see this melodramatic face of yours every day?"

"Ha. Ha."

I chuckled in spite of myself, thankful I got to process

this kind of stuff with her, despite her teasing. But it didn't take long for the reality of how soon things would be changing to settle over us again. She and Trev would be a married couple living in Portland by the end of the month. I'd be here alone until we graduated. Who knew what would happen after that?

She looped an arm around my shoulders. "Everything's gonna work out exactly as it should. Give it time."

I smiled at the all-too-familiar phrase. "You sound like my dad."

"Oh, Em, I'm so sorry. I didn't even think about how hard it must be, knowing he won't be there."

I blew my bangs away from my eyes. "Honestly, I've tried not to dwell on it too much yet. I've been more concerned about Riley. I don't want both of us to be separated from our dads that day. It's not right. Not when Mr. Preston can still be a part of our lives."

I swiped a T-shirt from the laundry basket and folded it on my lap. "Something broke this last time we were at their house. I felt it. I just wish I could—"

"Give it time," Jaycee said again.

I tossed the folded shirt onto the coffee table. "Time isn't exactly on my list of allies at the moment."

A knock on the door drew both our heads toward it. Jaycee hopped up first. Riley smiled at her as he stepped in, but it didn't reach his eyes. My pulse twitched. What now?

He nodded behind him. "Em, you have a sec?"

I flashed Jaycee an I-told-you-so look as I followed him into the stairwell.

"What's wrong?"

He didn't have to answer. The suitcase on the floor said enough.

"You're leaving?"

"Only for a few weeks." He backed against the railing. "Brett called. Said I don't have a choice in this one."

"I thought Brett was supposed to be taking care of things."

"He was. *Is*. But Nick dragged some high-dollar lawyer into the mess." Riley pushed off the railing, faced the ceiling, and heaved in a breath. He looked at me a minute later, confidence back in place. "I have to record this last song and wrap up the album. That's all. I'll be back in time for Jaycee's wedding."

I dipped my head to the side and raised an unconvinced brow.

He shuffled toward me. "I promise."

No telling what kind of leverage Nick and Jess would come up with to keep him there, but maybe that was what Riley needed. I gripped the bottom of his pullover. "If you need to stay longer, stay. I'm not going anywhere."

He slipped his hand behind my ear, and his smile repeated everything his eyes already told me. "I love you," he said anyway. He kissed my forehead. "Always."

No matter what followed, that was all I needed to know.

23

AWAITED

JAYCEE SWAYED with Trevor in the banquet hall, caught up in the thrill and relief of just finishing the perfect wedding ceremony. Between the glow of her smile and the shimmer of her veil, she was a vision of every fairy tale come to life.

I stepped back from the doorway, shut my eyes, and breathed so deeply that my champagne colored dress tightened across my chest. I had made it down the aisle and back without twisting an ankle. I'd even managed to make it through Trevor's vows without melting into a complete puddle of tears. But watching the two of them now nearly broke the dam again.

Riley's absence didn't help. Daily phone calls had carried us through the last three weeks apart, and I couldn't have been more relieved he was finishing his album, even if it had kept him in Nashville longer than planned. But with the live wire of the emotions already surging today, his arms of security would've been a godsend.

If nothing else, at least he wouldn't have to watch me dance with A. J. I was already nervous about it enough. Standing there, waiting for the emcee to introduce us only made it worse.

A. J. leaned an arm into mine. "You look stunning, by the way."

I patted the top of my sculpted updo. "Must be the *Labyrinth* vibe I've got going on. I swear, that French hairdresser attacked my head with no less than fifty bobby pins this morning."

He scrunched his lips to the side and examined the masterpiece. "Hmm, it does have a certain goblin king feel."

I swatted his hand away. "Just trying to show you up, Mr. Hair Gel."

His laugh tapered. Head down, he twisted his cuff link. "You do that without even trying."

The rumble of conversations from inside the reception hall settled as the emcee took the stage. I latched on to A. J.'s arm and exhaled through my mouth.

He covered my hand with his. If he grinned any wider, his dimples would overrun his cheeks.

"Lose the smirk," I whispered. "It's just a dance."

"Maybe," he said. "But it's definitely going to be one to remember."

The emcee cued our entrance. I dug my fingers around A. J.'s cuff. *For Jae.*

Music and clapping led us inside. Each couple in the wedding party took our designated positions on the dance floor. Every eye in the room zeroed in on us like dozens of miniature spotlights.

A. J. loosened my grip from his sleeve. "Relax."

Easy for him to say. "You're not the one in three-inch heels."

A string quartet in the corner began the song we'd danced to in rehearsals a dozen times leading up to today. He took my hand and rested his other on my lower back. "Stop thinking. Just feel the music, remember?" He drew me close. "I've got you."

With the same confidence that carried him through every aspect of life, he guided us in perfect rhythm around the floor. Halfway through the song, that confidence spilled over to me. The audience dwindled out of focus as the music swept me into the joy of sharing this moment with my friends.

A. J. must've noticed. He brandished a look of hard-earned satisfaction. "Look at you," he mouthed.

Why did he have to be so gifted at making me smile?

He spun me around and drew me back in. Hearing him singing softly with the music took me back to the night we danced in Portland last December. My lashes squeezed back my tears. I owed him for his friendship more than I fully understood.

The song gradually ended. A. J. bowed at the same time the room lit up in applause. And just like that, the

216 | CRYSTAL WALTON

dance was over. The segment of Jaycee's wedding I'd been dreading for weeks was finally done.

We followed the rest of the wedding party across the floor to take our seats at the head table.

The sound of silverware clinking against a champagne glass quieted the banquet hall again. A. J. rose from his seat with a microphone. "I'd like to offer a toast to the bride and groom."

Steady and handsome in a matching tux, he gripped Trevor's shoulder.

"Every once in a while, we're fortunate enough to experience the kind of friendship that defies time. Even though I've only known Trev for the last couple of years, I count him as a brother. He's taught me what it means to love without regret, fight with courage for my dreams, and learn when to surrender with grace." His gaze roamed to me.

"Trevor and Jaycee have shown me how every moment spent waiting for the one you're meant to spend your life with is worth the wait. So, today we honor their love, their friendship, and their commitment to the journey still ahead." A. J. raised his glass higher in the air. "To Trevor and Jaycee Andrews."

A collective, "Cheers," rang across the hall from table to table.

Rehearsing my own toast in my head, I stared at the bubbles climbing the edge of my glass until Jaycee's discreet nudge brought the microphone into view. I pushed my chair back to stand up. "I'd like to toast to my two best friends, whose friendship I'm fairly confident I never would've survived college without."

The audience laughed on cue. If Riley were there, I would've found his eyes in the crowd and latched on to the reassurance they always provided. But he was where he needed to be. And right now, so was I—surrounded by Dad's promise of the good things in store for me. Good friendships included. The kind that had taught me so much about love and grace.

"If you've known Jaycee and Trevor for long, you know today doesn't mark the end of one season or the start of another. It's a continuation of the commitment they've shared all along."

I angled toward them. "Throughout your marriage, may you always have the humility to admit when you're wrong, the discernment to know when love requires no words at all, and the joy to keep you laughing through every step along the way." I clinked my glass with theirs. "To my best friends. I love you both."

Trevor and Jaycee exchanged the briefest glance before simultaneously jumping from their seats and engulfing me in a two-person hug.

"Need... to... breathe," I choked out with a laugh.

Truth be told, I didn't want to let go—of them or of the moment. As soon as they released me, the night swept them up in a whirlwind of joy. From dinner to dancing to time spent at each table, the happy couple barely sat down for the rest of the reception.

As guests pushed back plates of half-eaten wedding

cake and gathered their things to leave, I ran my fingers along the gift table and took in the end of Jaycee's dream day.

Someone grabbed my hand from behind. "C'mon, you're going to miss it."

A. J. towed me toward the front of the building and into an immersion of bubbles floating through the air. A glimpse of Jaycee's back sparkled through the crowd right before a car door closed her in.

I pushed through the rows of people. "Wait." I hadn't gotten to say goodbye.

The tires screeched as Trevor gunned away from the church. I found a break in the crowd to the left and jogged after them in my heels, but it was too late. Stopping in the middle of the street, I braced my hands against my knees.

Brake lights flashed. Jaycee hopped out before the car came to a complete stop, ran over, and whirled her arms around me. "I love you so much. Thanks for everything today."

I squeezed her back. "Love you, too, Jae. Have a great time."

With a wink of nervous excitement, she twirled around and jogged back up to the car waiting to whisk her away to her long-awaited honeymoon.

The group in front of the church disbanded in various directions to their own cars. Though drained, I wasn't quite ready to leave yet.

I lifted the hem of my dress and walked along the side of the building toward a deck overlooking a lake.

The back door closed behind a couple reentering the banquet hall as I rounded the corner. Other than the faintest trail of voices from inside, stillness hovered over the deck. I rested my arms on the wooden rail, drank in the sunset's rich orange glow covering the water, and listened to the evening's lullaby in the surrounding woods.

Leave it to Jaycee to find such a stunning property.

"They made it."

I turned toward A. J.'s voice.

From the corner of the building, he strolled across the deck. He kept his hands in his pockets, holding open the sides of his unbuttoned tuxedo jacket. Both ends of his undone bowtie lay flat against his white shirt. Poor guy looked almost as exhausted as I felt.

I peered across the lake again. "Yep. After all this time, they finally made it."

A. J. tapped his elbow against my arm and angled his head in my direction. "I hear weddings are supposed to be happy occasions."

"They're my best friends. Of course I'm happy for them."

As usual, he grinned in response to the reaction he got out of me, but it didn't last. "And what about you?" he said slowly. "Are you happy?"

I closed my eyes and searched for an honest answer. "Yes and no. It's just that this is it, you know? This is the beginning of everything changing. We're all starting new chapters in our lives."

"Is that a bad thing?"

I shrugged. "Just different, I guess." I turned from the glassy water. "I don't know if I'm ready to say goodbye to it all."

A. J.'s eyes creased. "Some things are harder to let go of than others."

"Especially when you're afraid of what you'll lose," Riley said from behind us.

A PAGE TURNED

RILEY PUSHED off the brick wall. I wasn't sure how long he'd been standing there or how much he'd overheard, but his face didn't show anything other than affection.

He headed toward A. J. and me with his suit jacket draped over his arm, tie loosened around his neck, and eyes radiating above his blue dress shirt.

By this point in the evening, my hair had to be a tangled mess. No telling what kind of smudge marks my mascara had left under my eyes. Yet Riley still looked at me as though I took his breath away.

He edged close to kiss my cheek. "I told you no one would be looking at your feet."

"You made it."

He kept his eyes on mine. "Promised I would."

A. J. backed away, but Riley held out an arm to stop him.

If I could've slithered through the railing slats and

222 | CRYSTAL WALTON

hidden under the deck, I might've. They hadn't spoken since Riley first came back from Nashville in December. And after such a draining day, I wasn't sure I could handle the confrontation.

A. J.'s stare strayed from me to Riley and equaled his intensity.

The silence swelled around my vocal cords.

Riley didn't lower his gaze. "It'd be naive to pretend I don't know your friendship means a lot to Emma. You were there in times when she needed a good friend."

The unexpected tenderness in his voice tightened my throat even more.

A. J. squared his shoulders, probably steeling himself for whatever he thought was coming next.

Riley looked away, half smiled, and kneaded his neck. "It'd also be naive to pretend your connection with my fiancée doesn't make me insanely jealous." He laughed softly before raising his head again.

"But I've had to learn that loving Emma means trusting and respecting her heart, even if it means risking my own. All I'm asking..." He paused and gazed at me so long, I wasn't sure he was going to finish. A slow blink returned his focus to A. J. "All I'm asking is for you to do the same."

A. J. stared at the lake. Jaw clenched, he sucked in a breath and forced down whatever response had almost come out.

I don't know how much time passed in the silence, only that things felt lighter somehow. A slight smile touched A. J.'s face as he nodded at Riley in what resembled a bow of surrender. Without saying anything, he shuffled backward, turned, and disappeared into the banquet hall.

He'd grown more than he realized.

I curled into Riley's arms.

When a chill swept through my spaghetti strap dress, he draped his suit jacket over my shoulders. "You okay?"

"You mean, besides my feet?" I stepped out of my heels and stretched my ankles.

Riley tipped my chin until my eyes met the genuine concern in his.

I forced a weak smile. "I'm good. A little emotional. That's all."

"Not everything's gonna change."

How did he always know what I was thinking?

"You'll still have your best friend. She'll just be your *married* best friend."

"Thanks for that clarification." I hunched over the railing again. "It's gonna be strange though. Being in the apartment all by myself."

From behind me, Riley placed his hands on my shoulders and rested his chin on my head. "Good news is, you'll be getting a new roommate soon. I doubt he'll be as neat as Jaycee, but I hear he makes a pretty good pot roast. Assuming he can wean you off your frozen-meal-in-a-bag dependence."

Shaking my head, I pressed my back against his chest. "I guess living with you won't be *that* bad."

"Well, that's a relief. I was worried marriage might not live up to your expectations. But if you'll settle for it being *not that bad*, then this should be a piece of cake."

I elbowed him, but he only held me tighter. "It's interesting, though, isn't it?"

I circled toward him. "What is?"

"Life. It's like we're always given exactly what we need to make it through each little part." He stared past me into the woods and into thoughts that sounded like they were forming as he spoke.

Earnest transparency met my eyes again. "I don't know what this next season will look like, Em. I don't know where we'll end up or how long it'll take to get there. But I know we've been given each other. And honestly, that's enough."

A hundred thoughts surged, but only one mattered. "I love you."

Riley's fingers glided across my temple and dove into my hair. His smile slid to the left. "Just so you know, fear of Jaycee's wrath is the only thing keeping me from running down to that altar with you right now."

My laughter deepened his expression. He eased even closer, gaze drifting to my lips. I clung to his sleeve. It didn't make a difference how many times I'd told myself a look wasn't an actual kiss. His eyes always said otherwise.

The wood railing creased into my lower back. I wove my fingers through his hair and ran my other hand down his lapel.

He rested his forehead against mine. "We better get away from this church."

I didn't argue. Not that he gave me the chance. I barely had time to snatch my shoes up from the ground before he had me flying around the building toward his Civic.

A few miles down the road, his car slowed to a stop beside the forest. "C'mon."

I looked down at my dress. He couldn't be serious.

He jogged around the front bumper and opened my door. He *was* serious. Perfect. I shoved my shoes back on, took his hand, and followed him down a narrow trail cluttered with overgrown ferns. "A little farther," he called behind him.

"Wait, you've been here before?"

He smiled over his shoulder. "Just warming you up to surprises."

Why did his grin have to be so ridiculously charming?

He turned and jogged backward a few strides ahead of each of mine.

"Riley, I swear, you're…"

The moon's reflection shimmering over the lake stopped me short the minute we stumbled out of the woods. Riley kept jogging down to the shoreline and beamed at me the way he had when he'd first shown me the clearing in the woods near Reed.

I waded through the sand to his side. "How'd you find this place?"

"You have no idea how long you guys were taking pictures earlier, do you?"

"When did you get here? I didn't see you."

He shrugged. "Surprises aren't fun if you know about them."

I pinched his side. "You're lucky I'm in heels right now."

His laughter petered into a look of sobriety. He reached for my hand, eyes never leaving mine. "I think it's only fair I get a dance too."

"Here?"

His smile answered for him. Of course he meant here. I freed my ankles from my heels.

Between the wind rustling through the trees and the crickets playing their usual symphony, our secluded stretch of moonlit beach couldn't have been a more perfect dance floor.

Barefoot in the sand, I clung to his arms and the beginning of a new chapter in my life. "You know, you're right. About what you said earlier." I set my chin on my hand over his shoulder. "We're always given exactly what we need along the way."

"My brave fiancée." He leaned back and looked down like he was wrestling over how to say something.

He hadn't said what happened in Nashville. My stomach dropped at the possibilities.

His lashes swept toward mine. "I'm glad you're feeling brave, because there's something I need to tell you."

I pulled back from his arms. "Your contract? Is every-thing okay?"

"For now."

"Oh, that's comforting."

He waved it off. "The album's done. Brett's got some things in the works that have Nick eating out of his hand. That's not what we need to worry about."

"There's something else to worry about?" Would it ever stop?

Riley drew a line in the wet sand with his shoe. "I got a call from my mom last night." He swallowed as he faced me again. "They're coming to your graduation."

What?

He picked up a flat rock from the shore and turned it around in his hands. "Aside from having Jazz as your new shadow for a couple of days, it shouldn't be too bad."

I didn't buy it. "What aren't you telling me?"

He skipped the rock across the water. "Mom said my dad wants to talk to us..." He turned slowly. The lake didn't come anywhere close to the depth in his eyes right then. "About the wedding."

25

EXPOSED

BETWEEN GETTING USED to living in the apartment alone, poring over my final research paper, and dividing my roles at the center, two weeks of nonstop activity should've overshadowed the gnawing question of what Mr. Preston had to say to us. If he was planning on with-holding his blessing, did he really have to wait until grad-uation to tell us? That day would be emotional enough.

I twisted my necklace in a spiral and let it go. *One day at a time.*

Darius and Brandon came in from the basketball court with white paint flakes splattered on their arms and faces.

Trey sat up at his desk. "All done?"

Brandon spun his paintbrush in the air. "You should see it, yo. That court is sweet now." He and Darius clasped hands. "Alls I got to say is, those girls better be ready for a rematch." He strutted toward the classroom where a group of girls was working on a science project. "Once that paint dries, it's on."

They trailed into the room, and Trey rocked back in his chair. "How long do you think they'll last in there?"

"Thirty seconds tops."

My cell's ring cut into our laughter. I swiped the screen. "Jae?" She rarely ever called me at work.

"Are you near a computer?"

I shook my mouse. "Yeah. Why?"

"Go to KATU.com."

The local news station? My heart rate picked up. Whatever it was, it couldn't be good. I held the phone with my shoulder and typed in the URL.

"Middle of the page," she said. "See it? The ex-executive part?"

A picture of an officer leading a man into a patrol car came up in the headlines: *Ex-Executive Caught Defrauding Company.* The link pulled up a video feed. My pulse skipped again. "Jae, let me call you back." I motioned Trey over and clicked on the video.

The same reporter who'd waved her microphone around our faces that day someone had plastered the picture of Dee on the building stood in front of this guy's house now, looking extra makeup-y for the camera. "Earlier today, a local grant foundation exposed suspected fraudulent activity from one of their former executives, James Brake. These internal allegations are reported to have cost Brake his job and may lead to a jail sentence."

The shot zoomed in on two officers escorting Mr. Brake across the lawn. He bucked against them and strained for a view in front of the camera. "I was protecting this city's future. Keeping our streets clean." A haunted look in his eyes cut to my core. "For the next generation. We must pave the way for the next generation."

The taller cop got a tighter hold on him and led him into the police car. Behind them, a silver BMW sat in the driveway. I dropped my cell in my lap. Mr. Brake had been the one following me? The one who'd been black-mailing Mr. Glyndon? But I'd thought—

My phone rang again. I patted for it but couldn't take my eyes off the screen. "Hello?"

"Miss Matthews, it's Neal Chandler."

The name set off another jolt down my body. "Yes?"

Trey sat on the edge of my desk.

"I assume you saw the news?" Mr. Chandler asked.

I paused the video. "Just now, actually. I can't believe…"

"I didn't want to either. Jim was with us since the beginning. A little overzealous at times but committed. After his daughter was attacked, he—"

"Attacked? I thought someone only broke into her car."

"A few weeks after that, someone cornered her in a public parking lot downtown."

He didn't need to go into the details. It had to have been heinous enough to drive Mr. Brake this crazy. Despite my feelings toward him, my heart ached for his daughter. Especially after having been so close to a similar situation myself. I clutched my necklace.

Trey slanted me a what's-going-on look. I switched over to speakerphone and set my cell beside my keyboard.

Mr. Chandler coughed away from the line. "Jim's been a little off ever since then, getting sloppy with his work. I came across some errors, but I figured he was making mistakes from not being on top of his game. I never suspected it was intentional."

He had every right to feel blindsided. No one's ever prepared for betrayal.

"After I got your message, I did some digging. Turns out, he falsified reports to sway the board's decision on your proposal."

I grabbed Trey's hand and deflected a wave of anger. It wasn't Mr. Chandler's fault.

"We originally signed on because we saw potential in the center. And we'd like to make good on that decision." He cleared his throat, and I squeezed Trey's fingers even tighter.

"I have the check in my hands and will deliver it first thing tomorrow."

And I'd still be sitting here, trying to find my voice.

26

PAUSE

EVEN WITH THE relief of knowing the center had enough funding now to cover at least two years of expenses, life's nonstop churning didn't let up. I barely had time to remember how to breathe. Then there were other moments that made breathing completely irrelevant.

Still heady from a kiss, I lowered back down to my heels but kept my arms around Riley's waist. We were the only ones outside my apartment aside from two sparrows and a rambunctious squirrel rustling in a tree across the street. I savored the early spring air, still torn over moving on.

Riley studied me, as though reading a perfectly legible rendition of my thoughts. His boyish smile moseyed closer. "You're spending the night with your best friend. You're supposed to look excited."

"I am, but you sure you don't mind?"

We spent virtually every evening together. It felt sort of strange to be going somewhere without him. Not that Jaycee would've let me bring him. She'd been begging me the last few weeks to come to her new place for a girls' night. No guys allowed.

"Of course I don't mind. It'll be good for you. Besides," he said, "Jake and I are going to have a guys' night."

"Doing what? Sharing a Milk-Bone?"

He laughed. "Hey, don't knock 'em till you try 'em."

"Sick."

Riley drew me close and gave me one of those looks that cut through my attempt at hiding anything from him. "We have—"

"The rest of our lives. I know." A breeze whisked past us but lacked its usual comfort.

He lifted a hand to the back of my neck. No one should be allowed to have such unfairly disarming eyes.

"Em—" His cell rang from his pocket. This time, he answered. "Riley Preston." His gaze flicked away from mine toward the trees across the street. A second later, he let go of my fingers and strode in the opposite direction.

"Not gonna happen." He stopped on the curb with his back facing me. "Nick already knows my position on this. I'm not going without her... Look, I'll call him in the morning, but..." He clenched his fingers through his hair. "I'm sorry, Jess, but this conversation's over."

It took him a minute to turn around after hanging up. But when he did, a visible look of apology filled in for words.

He didn't need to explain. It made sense—at least to everyone but Riley—that he should start touring as soon as possible. It was also clear to everyone—apparently, even to Jess—that I was the one holding him back.

I started for him and the conversation we needed to have.

Again.

He flung his hand up. "Don't. I'm not leaving you."

"But—"

"But nothing. Touring can wait. You can't."

"I'm not going anywhere." Please tell me he didn't still question that.

"Neither am I." His tone left little room for negotiation. "You come first, Em. Always." He drew me back into the position we'd been in before Jess's interruption. "Everything's gonna work out."

"Will it?" I wanted so much to believe him.

He backed up. "Why do you keep doubting?"

His question caught me in the gut. I didn't have an answer. At least, not one I wanted to admit. I dragged the tip of my sneaker along the sidewalk divider.

"Em, there's nothing seen or unseen that's going to keep us apart. You know how I know?" Angling to meet my eyes, he waited until he had my complete focus. "When I was eighteen, I—"

Honk!

We both spun toward Jaycee's Fiat soaring up to the curb. She rolled down the passenger window. "Girl, you ready?"

Are you kidding me?

Chuckling, Riley brought my hands to his lips. "Go on. We'll talk later."

I would've made him finish talking right then if Jaycee would've let me get away with it. Giving in, I lifted on my toes to kiss him goodbye. "We're not done here."

Another laugh curled around me. "Have a good time tonight."

Once in my seat, I mindlessly fastened my seat belt, still caught up in the unfinished conversation.

Jaycee lowered her sunglasses down her nose. "What's wrong?"

I swear, it was like the girl had some invisible barometer that could assess the emotional climate of any situation in one point two seconds. "You sure you didn't sneak a counseling minor into your degree without telling me?"

She flaunted a grin bordering way too closely to Trevor's. "I tried, but they didn't believe me when I told them living with you for four years could pass as my hard-earned practicum."

I balled up a napkin from the door's side pocket and flicked it at her.

She dodged it with her palm while turning up the stereo.

If nothing else, she'd make tonight entertaining.

We'd made it through half of *Michael Jackson's Greatest Hits* by the time we reached her townhome in the heart of Portland. Jaycee unlocked the front door. "Wait 'til you see what I bought last weekend. You're gonna love—"

Her words, along with her entire body, skidded to a stop two feet inside. "Trev!"

In the living room, he and A. J. each sat in a Lazy Boy. Trevor waved in our general direction without unlocking his attention from the television screen. "We were just keeping the seats warm for you."

She toed her shoes off in the entryway. "Sorry, Em. We're supposed to have the house to *ourselves*," she said loud enough for the guys to hear.

Trevor, I could handle. But after seeing A. J. only a handful of times in passing since the wedding, his being there caused a weird sense of tension. At least, it did for me. He, on the other hand, looked completely undaunted. As usual.

Trev hopped up the second a commercial came on and whisked Jaycee in his arms from behind. "Don't worry. We're going to the pub on Fifth Street to watch the fight. You won't see us until the morning. Promise."

She caved, giggling in spite of herself, as soon as his lips met her neckline.

A. J. and I stayed on the outskirts of the kitchen, both

HOPE UNBROKEN | 237

looking around the apartment like we were performing some kind of building code inspection.

Jaycee finally maneuvered out of seduction territory. "What about your paper?"

Trevor grabbed a jacket off the coat rack mounted on the wall and slung his arms through the sleeves. "Tomorrow," he mumbled around the wallet pinched between his lips.

He stared at her scowl. "Oh, c'mon. You didn't seriously expect me to do schoolwork on a Friday night?"

Jaycee crossed her arms.

He turned to A. J. "Dude, help a friend out, here."

A. J. raised his palms in the air, claiming immunity. "Sorry, bro. I know better than to get in the middle of this one."

Trevor shoved him out the door. "How you gonna leave me flying solo like that?"

Thankfully, the unease left with them. Jaycee headed for the kitchen, huffing something that sounded like "boys." At the counter, she spun in her socks and bobbed her brows with enough excitement to eclipse Trevor's shenanigans. "Ready for a girls' night?"

No telling what she had planned. Without leaving me time to guess, she dragged out a dozen items from her cabinets until she'd covered half the countertop in a spread of goodies intended for a night of sweet oblivion. "I just got this old popcorn maker at a tag sale last weekend. Isn't it great? Very retro."

I fought back a laugh. She could've been a schoolgirl having her first slumber party.

"And what would girl time be without Starbucks hot chocolate?" She twirled around again with an array of flavored coffee liquors lined across her arms.

"Who'd you swipe those from?"

"I have my connections."

I broke open a container of sugar cookies. "You mean a husband who knows everyone on the planet?"

Jaycee turned on the teakettle. "Marriage does have its perks."

So did friendship.

This—this night, the spread, the laughs—was the perfect reflection of why I loved her so much. She couldn't have known how much I needed a night with my best friend. Or maybe she did. Although much had changed, some things never would.

I WOKE UP BEFORE JAYCEE—COURTESY of my internal alarm clock, which was forever set for seven a.m. After a quick shower, I crept down the hall. Aside from the soft hum of the pre-programmed coffeemaker, the house was soundless. I stopped at the edge of the living room.

Trevor had fallen asleep in one of the recliners with a game controller still in his hand and one too many drained energy drinks left on the coffee table. A. J. must've headed back to school last night.

Not wanting to wake anyone, I set my bag in the entryway, lugged Trevor's leather jacket over my arms, and slipped through the front door to greet the morning. A couple of steps onto the cold concrete stoop sent me jumping back to the welcome mat.

A gust of damp air rolled up the street. I tucked one side of the oversized jacket into the other and faced the sunlight cresting over the house across the street.

Standing there, I couldn't help daydreaming about the future—picturing what Riley and my house would look like, what it'd be like to wake up together every day.

I called his cell without another thought. It didn't occur to me until after the fourth ring that he might've still been asleep.

"Did I wake you?" I said as soon as he answered.

"No, I've been up for a while."

Something wasn't right. His tone was off, unsteady.

"Em, we need to talk. Listen, I—"

A sharp, grating voice filtered through the line.

"Who's that in the background?" I gripped the railing.

Riley exhaled. "I'm taking care of it."

"You didn't answer my question."

Not that it mattered. His deliberate pause said enough.

"What is she doing here, Riley?"

Another tense exhale. "Nick sent her."

I shed my jacket, all of a sudden burning up. "I'll be right there."

"Wait," he said. "We're not at my place."

"What?" Where else would they be?

Another pause stretched long enough to give my abs an entire workout.

"We're outside your apartment," he said slowly. "She didn't come to see me, Em. She came to see you."

27

SURRENDER

"I'LL BE RIGHT THERE," I repeated, weaker this time, and hung up. Instead of turning to go inside, I folded onto the porch steps with my arms wrapped around my legs and a marginal grasp on my phone.

What was Jess doing here? Did Nick have some new ultimatum to lord over us?

"I didn't expect to see you up this early," A. J. said from the end of the driveway.

I nearly jumped. "I thought you left."

"Had to get a run in first." He stopped short in front of the porch, looked behind him and back, and studied my face. "Everything all right?"

His emotional barometer was almost as attuned as Jaycee's.

I drew myself up by the railing. "I need to get back to campus."

"O-kay," he said in two drawn-out syllables. "I'll give you a ride. Let me grab my stuff real quick."

I followed him inside the house. He veered into the bathroom at the same time Jaycee emerged from her bedroom.

Led by her nose, she stumbled straight for the coffeemaker. "I was wondering where you were." She stared at me for a second before shuffling over to her mug on the counter. "What's wrong?"

Wow. I wasn't a completely open book or anything, was I? At least she'd understand.

"Jess is on campus."

Jaycee froze with her cup halfway to her mouth.

"She must've flown overnight. She came to see *me*, Jae. Not Riley. Me." My pulse skittered. No caffeine needed.

I twisted the bottom of my shirt into a coil. "I gotta go. There's no telling what kind of manipulation tactics this girl's gonna try."

Jaycee swirled another dash of creamer in her coffee. "I thought you wanted Riley to pursue his career."

"I did. I mean, I do. It's just... I have to get there." The fight in my voice was fading by the second. "I can't explain why."

She withdrew a traveler's mug from the cabinet. "All right. Give me a sec."

I didn't care who drove me home as long as we didn't waste any more time.

A. J. came down the hall with his hair rinsed and clothes changed. "Ready?"

"Jaycee's taking me."

Confusion morphed into concern as he looked between the two of us. "Someone want to tell me what's going on?"

A. J. was the last person I wanted to explain it to. I grabbed my bag and flew out the door.

"Long story," Jaycee said as she whirled past him.

Probably still half-asleep, she didn't say much on the drive. A single cup of coffee was barely a drop in the bucket for her. I didn't mind avoiding one of her psychoanalysis sessions, but the silence might've been even worse.

I managed to keep the deluge of *what if* questions at bay until we rolled up to the curb, and Jess came into view. I dug my fingers into the edge of the seat. "Who steps off a red-eye flight looking like one of Charlie's angels?"

Jaycee threw a hand over her mouth to block her laugh and tried to force a straight face. "Sorry."

If it were any other circumstance, I would've laughed with her.

I stole a quick minute to level out my shoulders. A deep breath helped me out of the car.

A. J. approached from one side while Riley hustled from the other, both faces creased with concern. Of course A. J. had come. And of course he'd beaten us. Why was I not surprised?

Riley closed in and looked from A. J. to Jaycee to me.

Jess sidestepped around him. "Emma, just the girl I've been waiting for." Her grating voice didn't hold a note of cordiality. She was here on business. Plain and simple.

I stared past her toward Riley.

She peered behind her shoulder. "Relax. I'm not here to steal your boyfriend."

Becky and Ashlea strolled up from the bottom of the hill with stacks of library books in their hands. It only took a second for Ashlea to latch on to the sight of a gorgeous woman standing less than a few feet away from A. J. Without even knowing what was going on, her eyes pinched with noticeable jealousy. After all this time of not hanging out with us anymore, she obviously hadn't let go of her feelings for him.

Jess fanned her straight blonde hair over her shoulder and stared at all of us as if we were a group of immature college students wasting her precious time. "I'm a businesswoman, Emma. I'm here because we need to sell records. And the only way we're going to sell records is if your boyfriend goes on tour."

Her heels stabbed the innocent concrete with each pointed stride toward me. "So, I need you to tell him you'll be just fine here without him."

Her patronizing, baby-talk tone was two seconds away from getting her slapped.

I looked at Riley again. One frustration bled into another. "I'm trying," I whispered.

Jess angled forward. "Try harder."

A. J. butted in and glared at her with quickly obtained animosity. "Why don't you back off?"

Riley stepped up. "I can handle this." His voice turned low but assertive.

A devilish grin followed Jess's back-and-forth glance between them. "Well, well," she practically sang. "I've underestimated you, Emma. You're good."

Riley wedged himself between us. "That's enough."

He stood tall and unmoving in front of her. Nobody else said a word. Jaycee grabbed A. J.'s forearm to keep him in place. Ashlea and Becky both cradled their books to their chests. And the tension kept me locked in the middle of it all.

The electric silence soared past ridiculous. Something inside me snapped and sent delirious laughter leaking out. If we had a few cameras, we could've been filming a reality TV show. I could hear Austin's narration now. He'd be mumbling something about drama and my being at the center.

I cracked. I couldn't help it. There were at least a dozen excuses I could've blamed it on, stress being top of the list. I laughed so hard I almost cried.

Bent over, I tried to wave it off. "I'm sorry." They probably thought I'd seriously lost it. Maybe I had. I struggled for composure as I trucked down the sidewalk.

Riley ran after me. "Em, hang on. Wait up a sec."

I tossed my hands in the air. "I'm done, Riley."

He stopped, worry stretching into panic.

I burrowed my fingers into my hair. "I'm done

wishing I had control over time. Done trying to figure this out and trying to force things to happen." Once my delirium drained away, the helplessness underneath had nothing left to hide behind.

"I can't convince you it's better to go back to Nashville any more than you can convince me it's better for you to stay. I'll support whatever choice you make, whether it delays our future together or not."

Sunlight clipped over the building behind Riley and caught a slow smile leading him toward me.

I held my ground. "I promised I was ready to spend my life with you—all of it. That doesn't mean after we get married. That means right now. Even if it includes being apart for a while."

Riley drew me close. "*That's* exactly why I'm staying." He kissed me slowly, obviously not giving a second thought to who was watching.

"I *will* take care of this, Em."

Drawing a breath, I nodded with complete acceptance. "I know. I trust you."

Trust. The word sank into my core as soon as I said it. This whole time, I'd been so desperate for him to trust me—to trust us, God's plans, His timing—all of it. But when it came down to it, I'd been letting doubt break my hope.

The endless unknowns that had been plaguing me roared in unison until, all at once, they quieted. A soft breeze stirred the leaves in the trees. Sunlight warmed my face. And in the most unlikely moment and place, a song of peace whispered over my spirit.

The tension of trying to work things out on my own seeped through my lashes in an act of surrender. The truth was unanswered questions would always be a part of me. I had no idea how Riley's contract would play out or what it'd mean for us. No clue how to leave behind the life I'd built here. I could barely think about making it to graduation, let alone what lay past it.

But the bigger truth was, I didn't have to know right now. I didn't have to see each step before it came or even where it was leading. I didn't have to be brave enough to get there or clever enough to make things happen. I needed to trust the One who was. If He'd shown me anything this last year, it was that He was trustworthy. And for that reason alone, I shouldn't have been striving in my own strength. I should've been resting in His.

Sometimes, I swore I was the slowest learner in the history of mankind. A glance to the sky ended in a repentant smile. I'd spent a lot of my life wishing away the clouds for fear of not being able to see the stars. But without storms, I'd miss the way showers of grace never failed to remind me just how tenacious love can be.

I squeezed Riley's hand, never so grateful for the way grace held me, even when I was still striving to understand it. "I'm gonna walk for a little bit. Clear my head."

Understanding touched his eyes. "I'll meet up with you in a while." He jogged back to where we left Jess and the others, and I headed in the opposite direction.

Walking had always been therapeutic for me, especially around the campus. Its familiar paths and secluded nooks were an inseparable part of my college experience —one I'd never forget and would always miss. Faithful as usual, the solitude welcomed me one more time.

The longer I walked, the more I accepted that life would likely never follow the road I had planned. But one thing I knew for sure. Regardless of which route we took or how long it'd take us to get there, Riley and I would walk together. Always. Through the delays and roadblocks. Through commencement, sorting out his record deal, and confronting Mr. Preston's decision about our wedding. We'd stand together even through the one event I still had no idea how I would ever survive.

28

LAST DANCE

WITH MY FINAL paper turned in and exams completed, I should've been riding the freedom wave. Two weeks of rushing through the start of May had quarantined Jess's failed mission to a cobwebby corner of my mind. Still, a grip of unrest wouldn't let me go. It had been mounting all semester. And the minute I walked into the center for my last day of work, I understood why.

I never dreamed I'd reach a day of wishing for more paperwork to do but staying busy was the only thing keeping me from losing it. The center had sown as much into me as I'd sown into it. Maybe more. It probably didn't make sense to be so attached after only a year, but it honestly didn't matter what logic said. My heart had a mind of its own.

Spending all morning trying not to cry in front of the kids took every ounce of energy I had. I'd chugged a bottle of iced tea after lunch and honed all my attention on to my office duties for the rest of the day. I jotted down every detail I could think of, leaving instructions for whoever'd be taking my place.

Aside from a few open-ended comments, Trey left me to my OCD behavior until Ms. Mendierez entered the office. He hovered beside my desk with a feigned look of surprise at her stopping by.

Ms. Mendierez inched her purse strap up her slender shoulder. "I can't stay long, but I wanted to be sure I told you." She looked down at her waitress uniform. "This is my last week at the diner. I got a new job."

I'd watched life return to her eyes over the last few months, but today they seemed more alive than ever. "That's awesome. Congratulations."

She tucked her hands inside her apron's front pocket and arched her shoulders. "I finally figured out what I want to do with my life, thanks to you. And when I heard there was going to be a vacant spot here, I just knew it was right."

My glance ricocheted from her to Trey and back. *Here?* The pieces came together more slowly than they should've.

Ms. Mendierez lifted her chin with a gained sense of dignity. "I may have lost my baby, but that doesn't mean I have to stop being a mama." She peered out the back door to the basketball court. "Those boys need someone in their lives to love on them, encourage their dreams." She faced me again. "I have big shoes to fill, Emma, but I'm willing to try."

It was the perfect fit for her. Nothing could've made me happier. The tears I'd been stifling all day almost won the war.

"And I'm not the only one you inspired. Mrs. Jackson did it," she said. "She opened her Mama's Café."

I couldn't speak. Couldn't blink. Positive if I moved at all, that'd be it. The avalanche would be relentless.

Trey lifted off the side of the desk and showered us with an intuitive smile. "It's amazing how many dreams are simply waiting for us to take that first step of faith."

Perspective. He'd never lost it. Not once. And of course, he'd been right all along.

"Well, then." Ms. Mendierez cleared her throat and dabbed the skin under her eye. "You take care of yourself, Emma." She held out a hand.

Without hesitation, I threw my arms around her instead and held on for longer than she was probably comfortable with. "You be strong and courageous."

With a slight quiver across her shoulders, she held me tighter. "For Dee," she whispered.

"For Dee."

She squeezed both my hands, smiled with her eyes, and strode for the door. I stayed at my desk and stared at yet another reminder of the legacy Dee's life had left behind.

A hint of the sunset streamed through the door slowly shutting behind her. The day was ending too fast.

I shoved down the thought. If I'd made it this long without crying, I could finish strong.

I dove into my work for another couple of hours and steeled myself a little more with each hug goodbye. By the time eight o'clock rolled around, my desk was officially spotless. There wasn't a single paper left to file or a voicemail to record.

Aside from Trey, everyone else had already left for the day. I strolled through the quiet building, brushing my fingers across furniture as I passed. Each desk. Each corner. I memorized every scene for fear they'd deteriorate with time.

I saved the basketball court for last. Even newly renovated, it still held too many memories to count. On the bench, I locked one arm under the other and leaned into the bricks.

It wasn't goodbye forever. I promised I'd see the kids every time I came in town to visit Jaycee and Trevor. It'd be okay. Wouldn't it?

"Thought you weren't supposed to be here alone," A. J. said from the fence.

I hooked a thumb toward the door. "Trey's inside. What are you doing here?"

He sauntered across the court with a lopsided grin. "Kids aren't the best at keeping secrets. They told me it was your last day."

Of course they did.

A. J. dropped beside me onto the bench. Chuckling, he reached for the paperclip pinning my bangs out of my face. "Rough day?"

"You could say that."

"I kind of figured it would be. Thought I'd swing by to make sure you were all right."

Head lowered, I tugged the zipper on my jacket up and down. "That's sweet. I'm fine, though. Really."

"Fine?" He made a face. "Mm-hmm."

"Okay, maybe a *tad* emotional."

He laughed. "Still trying to win those understatement of the year awards, huh?"

I shoved his shoulder, but he pressed his arm right back into mine. We sat there, side by side. No words. Just friendship, memories.

"I can't believe we're finally here," he said. "Graduation, I mean."

"Tell me about it. Seems surreal, doesn't it?"

A. J. stretched out his legs and crossed one ankle over the other. "Guess we can't suspend time, after all."

I tried not to snort. "Story of my life." I looked out toward the top of the court. How could four years have passed so quickly? "It drives us forward whether we're ready or not."

"Oh, I think we're ready." As usual, his voice rang full of confidence.

"You're that sure, huh?"

He lifted off the wall and angled toward me. "Sometimes you just know when it's the right time to move on."

Maybe. But letting go was the hard part. I gripped the edge of the bench. "So, what are you going to do after graduation?"

"Actually," he said, "I'm sticking around here."

His eyes told me *"here"* meant more than only Portland.

"Don't look so surprised. Trey's been asking me for a while to come on board full-time." He swiped off his baseball cap and ran his fingers through his hair. "It took me longer than it should've to figure it out, but my place is here with the kids."

"What about sports medicine?"

"Psh. The kids are way more entertaining than pro athletes."

We both laughed.

He shrugged. "Honestly, I think I've always known I wasn't going to do anything with sports med. It just took me a while to sort it all out."

"I know the feeling." I leaned my head against the bricks. "What about your dad?"

He tucked his hat back on. "He'll get over it eventually."

The trees on the other side of the fence shook in the wind and streaked a shadow across his face, along with a trace of pain.

Walking away from his dad's expectations couldn't have been easy. Maybe we were all a little braver than we thought.

He stared at the net opposite us. "After coming here, it was like—I don't know—like reaching a crossroads or something." He held one hand out to the side. "I could choose what the world considers success." He held out the other hand. "Or I could choose what I find most fulfilling."

He might as well have been reading straight out of my journal from last year.

"I'm glad you made the right choice." For him. For Trey. The kids. There wasn't a question in my mind that he belonged here.

A. J. lowered his chin. "I'm not sure I would've if it weren't for you."

Me?

"You've taught me a lot, Em. I know you don't see it, but it's true."

His sincerity added to the pang that'd been snowballing all day.

He broke the hold he had on my eyes and cleared his throat. "You've really outdone yourself on this one. The court looks amazing."

I couldn't argue with the second part. A freshly painted pole. New net. Clear lines on the pavement. There were even potted trees in each corner and baby ivy vines climbing the side of the fence facing the street.

"You'll have to thank the kids for that." I crossed the court, taking it all in. "This is *their* court now. They worked hard to earn it."

"It's yours too."

I bent and traced my initials carved into the base of the post. "It'll always be a part of me." I stayed there for another minute before strolling back to the bench.

"So, what about you?" he asked as I approached. "Where's life taking you after graduation?"

"Nashville. At some point anyway." I took my seat again. "Actually, I've been thinking. If there isn't already an organization there similar to the center, I might start one."

A. J. smiled. "Wouldn't have expected any less." He reached inside his jacket, withdrew a wrapped gift, and placed it on my lap. "An early graduation present."

"A. J., you didn't have to—"

"Just open it. You'll like it. Trust me."

Relenting, I peeled back the wrapping paper. "*Labyrinth?*"

"Don't worry. I didn't warn Riley about your thing for David Bowie." He looked from side to side and leaned forward to whisper. "It'll be our little secret."

I shook my head at him. My heart turned into a pinball machine with way too many emotions colliding into each other. I drew the DVD close. "Thank you," I whispered.

He dipped his chin and rose from the bench. "If you don't mind, I'd like to keep the Journey CD. For posterity."

"How can I deny a convert to eighties' music?"

Laughing, he extended a hand to help me up. "You were right about Jaycee." He grabbed his phone from his pocket and ran a thumb over the screen. "She definitely didn't go for me changing up her wedding plans." He set his cell on the bench and faced me again. "But maybe we can have that dance now. Friend to friend. One last time."

His eyes didn't hold the same smoldering look they had in the past. Only friendship—one I treasured.

The entire court filled with the sound of "Open Arms" as we shared the final dance in this chapter of our lives.

So much for making it through the whole day without crying. The weight of it all soaked into the front of A. J.'s jacket.

Not that he'd ever let me drown. He held my hand and twirled me across the ground. Instead of tripping over my feet, I spun with grace and stopped on perfect cue.

He raised a brow. "Those dance lessons paid off."

I twirled in and landed my back to his chest like a seasoned ballroom dancer. "Someone once taught me how to dance with *swag*."

He cracked up. "You got it, Dancing Queen. Dee'd be quite proud." A. J. circled me around toward him.

I returned my chin to his shoulder and swayed with the music.

"I mean that, Em," he said. "Dee'd be proud of all you've done for the center and the way you've grown as a person."

I wasn't the only one who'd grown. I clutched the back of his jacket. "How am I supposed to say goodbye to all of this?"

"You're not really letting go," he said. "The friendships you've made here, the experiences you've gone through. They're part of who you are now. They'll go wherever you go."

His words squeezed around the piece of my heart his life had forever impacted. "I'm not sure that's how it works."

"Of course it is." He leaned back slightly. "You see me now, right? Just take that image with you." His gaze trailed over my face. "Memories are like photos. You pull them out any time you want. All you have to do is close your eyes. It's almost real."

Almost real. "But not enough." I faced the stars, overwhelmed with the memories of all we'd gone through together, of how much had changed. "I love you, A. J." I always would.

He rested his cheek against my temple. "But not enough," he whispered.

Our journey over the last two years had caused that truth to stretch deep enough in both our hearts to a place where it could finally heal.

He kissed my cheek as he let go. "C'mon. I'll walk you to your car."

I stopped at the fence and turned one last time. A. J. was right. It was time to move on. But I didn't leave the center, saying goodbye. I left that night, taking it with me.

Back at my apartment, I removed my keys from the knob and swung the door shut with my foot. The floor-length curtains in the living room waved in a breeze from the window.

"Hey, Em," Jaycee said from a seat at the kitchen table.

I jumped a foot in the air.

"Hope you don't mind. I let myself in."

"I see that. Thanks for the heads up." I dropped my purse on the stand beside the door and traipsed toward the smell of mint hot chocolate.

"Trev and I wanted to stay on campus tonight. Didn't seem right not being here the night before graduation."

"Trev's staying with A. J.?"

"Yep." She scooped a hefty spoonful of whipped cream off the top of her mug. "You sure you want to move to Nashville? I don't think I can handle the two of them together without some kind of female rein-forcement."

I laughed at her contorted expression. "Wish I could, but Riley's dreams are too important to me."

Jaycee raised her spoon in the air. "And that, girl-friend, is what's going to make you the amazing wife I know you're going to be."

"Spoken from an expert." I joined her at the table.

She tilted her chair on its back two legs and spread out her arms like she was about to burst into song. "I'm telling you. Marriage is amazing. Never having to say good night, getting rid of all those stupid insecurities, knowing you're committed to each other for life... There's nothing like it."

Her chair dropped forward. "I'm so excited for you to experience this, I can hardly stand it."

And I could hardly stop laughing at the lingering effects of her honeymoon stage. "Well, I can't think about that yet. I gotta get through tomorrow first." With trying to get through everything else this semester, I'd set wedding planning aside for after graduation. I was leaving most of it up to Jae anyway.

"Tomorrow? Why are you worried about tomorrow?"

"You mean, other than walking across the stage in front of hundreds of people—which, by the way, I'm already planning on wearing flats, so don't even think about trying to coerce me into wearing heels."

She started to roll her eyes but stopped herself when they landed on my hair.

"Jae..."

"What?" She feigned a look of innocence.

I waved a finger at her. "Whatever's going through your mind right now, you can forget it."

"Em, if you refuse to wear heels, you at least have to let me do your hair." She poked me in the side. "It'll be fun," she said in a perfect rendition of Trevor's obnoxious voice.

Maybe it would be. As long as whatever Mr. Preston had planned didn't ruin it all.

29

CHANGED

AT THE FOOT of the platform, I tried to ban "Pomp and Circumstance" from my head while watching the student in front of me climb the stairs.

"Emma Marie Matthews."

I couldn't have walked more than twenty feet across the stage. Yet in that short span, my entire college experience scrolled through my mind in a slideshow of memories. The provost shook my hand as a camera snapped in front of us.

One flash. One blink. And it was over. This chapter of my life, closed. My identity as a college student, terminated. But as I carried the cylindrical placeholder across the rest of the stage, I smiled knowing I walked away with something I'd finally learned to cherish.

Time.

Another series of flashes greeted me at the bottom of

262 | CRYSTAL WALTON

the short staircase. Riley bent over the barrier. "Told you you're braver than you think you are."

A staff worker with sweat drizzling down his temple redirected me back on course before the next graduate in line bumped into my heels.

Mom and Austin weaved through the crowd up to where Riley stood behind the rail. "I'm so proud of you," Mom called.

I waved over my shoulder on my way back to my seat. Name after name blared from the podium, each tied to a student's culminating chapter of a much larger story. Some I knew well. Others were mere acquaintances. And some were unfamiliar names I'd likely never hear again. But right then, we were one. The final charge ended in a pandemonium of celebration from students, professors, and family members.

Lost in the crowd sprawling over the field, I tried not to tilt the cap Jaycee had secured this morning with an entire can of hairspray and a dozen bobby pins.

"You did it." A. J. prodded me in the shoulder as he came up from behind.

"Without tripping no less."

He motioned to the certificate in my hand. "They know talent when they see it."

I swatted him with it. "Must be why they gave you an award for crossing without that big head of yours throwing you off balance." I tugged on the tip of his cap, grateful for how good it felt to be at ease. Not only in that moment, but with A. J., period. Something had changed between us.

Riley maneuvered through the crowd and almost ran into me. Without slowing, he spun me off the ground and kissed me with such passion, it took a minute to regain my balance when my feet finally touched the grass.

"Wow, I'll walk across a stage any time if that's the greeting I get afterward."

"Sorry. I might be slightly on the proud side right now."

"I see that."

He steadied my tassel. "I have a graduation present for you, but it isn't exactly something I can wrap."

My stomach dropped without warning.

His excitement soared past any question written on my face. "I talked with Nick this morning. The tour's booked for the fall. I have to move back to Nashville in July, do some local venues until October, but everything's settled."

One blink. Two. "What about Jess? When she came, she made it sound like—"

"She came on her own. Nick didn't send her."

What?

His smile quickly obliterated all traces of his frustration with Jess. "Brett came through. He's been working on a new tour lineup since December. You're not gonna believe this, but the delay actually ended up opening a chance to tour with Tim McGraw." Riley squeezed his neck and laughed. "Nick's totally playing it up like he had it planned all along."

My jaw refused to work. Was this real? All of it worked out in even better ways than we could've planned for?

The memory of Dad's voice rushed over me. *"God has good things planned for your life—good friendships included. He's always leading us to good, Em. Even when we have to walk through things we don't understand. Sometimes, we just need to give Him a little time."*

I hedged back my tears.

Mom came up behind Riley. "There's my baby girl." Streaks of mascara trailed her cheeks as she cupped both sides of my face. "My little girl, all grown up."

"Mom."

She curved her arms around my back and sniffled against my shoulder. "I'm sorry. I promised myself I wouldn't do this."

Austin strolled up beside her. "How much did you have to pay the registrar's office to let you walk?"

"Cute, Aust." I raised my honor stole from my gown. "I hear they don't give you these sashes for no reason."

"Trying to compete with your big brother?"

"I think you can leave that to me," Anna said from behind him.

I stared from her to Austin and back. "Wait a sec. Are you two…?"

He shrugged. "Sometimes you don't realize what you want 'til it's right under your nose."

I jabbed his side. "Ha! I knew you'd be good for each other. Didn't I tell you?"

"You're bound to be right occasionally. Law of probability."

"Wow. I think this day might be one to mark in the history books."

Austin dished my grin right back at me. "As the day you won the award for being the most dramatic girl on campus?"

"Except that'd be the same as any other day," Trevor said out of nowhere.

I swore that boy had some kind of homing device that drew him to every opportunity to tease me.

"But we wouldn't trade you or your melodramatic flair for anything in the world." Jaycee squeezed my shoulder and turned to give my mom a hug. "Hi, Mrs. Matthews."

"Hi, sweetie." She looked at Jaycee and Trevor. "Now, aren't you two charming. How's marriage treating you?"

As the three of them fell into conversation, A. J. and Riley stood side by side on the outskirts in another reminder of how much we'd all grown.

"Pictures, Em." Mom flagged me over. "You and Jaycee first."

Trevor cradled his arms to his chest like he had hold of an imaginary teddy bear. "Aw... BFFs."

"Oh, stop that and get over there." Mom pushed him forward.

He barreled toward us, dragging A. J. along with him.

The two of them dove straight in between us. No telling what kind of faces they were making each time the camera flashed.

"Now, one of you and Riley, sweetheart."

I sank into Riley's side, not needing any prompting whatsoever to smile.

Swept up in Trevor's arms, Jaycee laughed. "You better get used to smiling, Em, or your cheeks are going to be hurting on your wedding day."

It didn't seem fair for the Prestons to crest the top of the hill at the exact moment the words "your wedding day" left Jaycee's lips. I reached for Riley's hand, torn between wanting to put this off and being way past ready to have it over with.

Jasmine glued herself to Riley before the rest of the family reached us. He managed to pry her off his legs, but she simply transferred her hold to his neck instead. He laughed. "Good to see you, too, Jazz."

"I missed you guys so much." She surveyed the distance between Riley and me, as though calculating how far she could stretch her arms to hug both of us at the same time.

Riley made the choice easy for her. He rose to his feet but only made it a few steps forward before another embrace almost knocked him over. Melody veered to his side so Mrs. Preston could have a turn as well.

Taking advantage of the distraction, Jasmine lifted on her toes to whisper in my ear. "I couldn't find a way to sneak my dress with us."

I feigned a look of shock that she, of all people, couldn't get something past her dad.

She grinned. "I know, it's hard to believe, but I snuck some pictures with me instead. They're on the camera Mom brought. I'll show you later."

I returned her wink of secrecy.

While Austin and Mom were getting acquainted with Mr. and Mrs. Preston, another face joined our crowd.

Trey held his arms open. "Congratulations. I always knew you'd go places, Miss E," he said in a tone he'd copied from the kids. "Just don't be forgetting us when you get there."

I squeezed him back. "Like that's possible."

His throaty laugh wrapped around me in a hug of its own. I held on a little longer until I was positive the sound sank far enough in my memory that I wouldn't lose it. Ever.

"You take care of yourself, kid." He patted my shoulder and offered a final flash of that ornery smile I would miss seeing every week. "Come back and visit us."

"I promise."

Trey clasped A. J.'s hand. Already caught up in conversation, they drifted down the hill through the maze of people toward the parking lot.

The center was in good hands. I breathed in, counted to ten, and exhaled. The last thing I needed was to lose my composure in front of Mr. Preston.

He was right in front of me when I turned around

again. Caught off guard, I had to force myself not to flinch.

He gestured to my robes. "Riley wasn't exaggerating when he said you were top of your class."

I waved it off. "He overestimates my abilities."

"I'd wager he thinks you overestimate his as well." Mr. Preston laughed at the confession written on my face. "I suppose that's what happens when you're in love. You become each other's biggest fan."

Was this conversation actually happening right now?

Riley glanced over at us. He set a hand on my mom's arm. "Excuse me for a minute."

"And you become a bit overprotective," Mr. Preston added when Riley practically sprang to my side.

Riley eyed him carefully.

"I was just congratulating Emma on a job well done," his dad said.

Not a single muscle on Riley's face moved.

Mr. Preston placed a hand on my shoulder and smiled. "If your father were here, I have no doubt he'd be very proud of you."

I might've been able to speak if I could've breathed. Instead, I simply stood there, arms at my side, staring into the kind of look a father held for his daughter.

Good thing Jasmine was there to hijack my near meltdown. She played with the edge of my oversized robe sleeve. "Do you think Reed will accept me?"

"They'd be crazy not to," Riley said.

Melody ruffled the top of Jasmine's hair the way

Austin sometimes did to me. "She's gotta make it through high school first." She scrunched her face at Riley. "You shouldn't egg her on."

He mimicked her pose. "And you shouldn't discourage her."

I knelt to the grass, unpinned my cap, and placed it on Jasmine's head. "There's nothing wrong with dreaming early." I caught Austin's grin on my way back up.

Mom stood a few paces in front of him and Anna. "We're going to head back to the hotel." She closed me into another tender hug. "We'll see you tomorrow, honey."

"Bright and early." I kept my smile in place until the car turned out of view. As much as I loved San Francisco, I didn't want to think about going home for any length of time.

Mrs. Preston grabbed Jasmine's hand and stretched her other arm around Melody's shoulders. "We're going to take a quick tour of the campus. I think my girls want to follow in their big brother's footsteps."

They headed toward the campus center, away from my last chance at putting off the conversation now staring us in the face.

Mr. Preston stashed his hands in his pockets. Coins rustled against the awkward silence until he cleared his throat. "I suppose you two know what I'd like to talk with you about."

Riley edged forward, my body safely guarded behind

his. "Dad, before you start, I need you to know Emma is the most important thing in my life. You may not have the highest estimation of me, but I'm ready to love her with everything I am. It's important to her that we receive your blessing for our wedding." He peered back at me and then squared off again. "Please don't deny her that honor."

Mr. Preston's stern expression didn't fade.

How could there be no air outside?

"It's important only to Emma?" he said slowly.

Riley didn't break eye contact. "No, sir." He squared his shoulders. "It's important to both of us."

Mr. Preston nodded, looking like he was about to dive into whatever speech he'd prepared.

I skirted around Riley. "Mr. Preston, please, I want you to know—"

He raised his hand. "That's quite all right, Emma. You've already made your love and devotion to my son more than obvious." He faced both of us. "I have no reason to doubt either of your commitment to each other."

He returned his focus solely to me with an expression I didn't understand. "You remind me of Rose when she was your age. Stubborn, vibrant, full of life. You're not afraid to go after what you want." His smile saddened. "Or make sacrifices for the one you love."

Riley's back straightened. "Emma isn't Mom. And I'm not you."

Mr. Preston's rueful smile overtook his eyes. "No, no

you're not." He moved toward me. "Sacrificial love certainly isn't a bad thing. Just be careful not to let Riley chase his dreams so far that he loses sight of the more important things."

He looked away, but not before the regret on his face tore through. "I've made my share of mistakes. Not the least of which was allowing my shame to shut my only son out of my life." Drawing a deep breath, he turned to Riley. "I wanted you to see me as the successful musician I longed to be. Someone you could look up to. Instead, I pushed you away."

A tendon on Riley's neck twitched as he swallowed. "I didn't want a musician. I just wanted a dad."

"I know." His chin drooped. "I drove you hard because I didn't want you to end up like me." He raked his fingers through his hair the way Riley did when he was frustrated. "When you gave up on music, you took away the one thing I used to keep from facing my own failures. I had nothing left to hide behind."

His shoulders caved another inch. "Except anger. I fought to let it go, but when you came back at Christmas, I realized I was still too afraid to." Mr. Preston braved a glance in our direction without raising his head. "I know I didn't show it, but your sisters have taught me a lot about what it means to be a father. I'm just sorry it was too late."

I gripped Riley's sleeve, silently begging him to tell his dad there was still time, but Riley didn't speak.

Mr. Preston swished the coins around in his pocket

again. "I can't change the past, but I wouldn't be the kind of father I always wanted to be if I denied you happiness." He withdrew his hands and stood tall. "I'll give you my blessing on one condition."

Riley's body tensed against mine.

Face completely softened, his dad smiled. "I'll consent to your wedding, if you'll allow me to have a part in the ceremony."

Every imagined condition that'd raced through my mind in those few seconds seeped out in a sigh. Relief pooled over every muscle. Until I looked up at Riley.

A statue of resolve, he flexed his jaw.

Mr. Preston's smile fell, along with my heart.

"Having my dad make some small appearance at my wedding isn't good enough." Riley placed a hand over his dad's sunken shoulder and met his eyes. "I need him where he always should've been. Right beside me."

A dozen different emotions touched Mr. Preston's expression during the minute it took him to respond. He raised his chin and gripped Riley's shoulder in return. "It'd be my honor."

The space between them collapsed into possibly the longest awaited hug I'd ever witnessed.

Mr. Preston blinked away any evidence of tears and straightened out the front of his dress shirt. "I better go find my girls before Rose writes a check for two enrollment deposits."

He stopped midway in a turn but then kept trekking

down the hill, fading from a moment that had just changed everything.

I took his place in front of Riley. "Now who's the brave fiancé?"

He shrugged it off.

"I'm serious. It took a lot of courage for your dad to own up to his mistakes. And even more for you to give him grace. I know that wasn't easy."

Riley exhaled. "We've had too many wasted years. I'm tired of what insecurities have cost us all." His forehead creased. "But listen, about what he said earlier. We don't have to go to Nashville."

"Yes, we do." It was time to move on.

"I don't ever want to put my music above you."

"You won't."

Uncertainty stole the usual confidence in his eyes. "How can you be sure?"

"Because I know *you*." I lifted a hand to his unshaven cheek. "And I won't let you forget who you are." My promise melded into a kiss I didn't want to release. Love was enough. It would carry us through the summer, through moving to Nashville and building both our dreams there, and even through whatever time apart we'd have to spend while he toured.

He smiled against my lips. "You know, I just realized we have absolutely nothing holding us back now. Technically, we can get married whenever you want. Even before June."

"How about right now?" I said, still recovering from that kiss.

He threw his head back. "Tempting, but I doubt we can plan a whole wedding in a couple of hours."

"Ah, don't underestimate the matron of honor. She's a pro."

Riley laced his fingers around my lower back. "Maybe we should start with choosing the location. Do you know where you want to have the ceremony?"

As much as I wanted to get married, I hadn't given much thought to the details. They'd seemed so inconsequential. Until right now.

"Actually," I answered slowly. "I think I do."

ALWAYS

THANKFULLY, Jaycee had the summer off as a teacher and was able to come to Lake Tahoe for an extended visit. Few people were fortunate enough to have their own personal wedding planner for free, especially one who was a miracle worker. In only three weeks since her arrival, we had every detail solidified from the ceremony to the reception.

Jaycee wasn't the only one whose natural talents had come into play. Melody thrived at being in charge of coordinating the music for the whole weekend.

Without any girls of her own, my aunt was delighted to open up their lake house to us and share in the excitement with my mom.

Even Mrs. McAllister had come down to help Jaycee with the finishing touches. As with Jaycee's wedding, the project seemed to boost her mom's spirits. I wouldn't have known she was sick at all if it weren't for the regiment of medicine she had to take throughout the day.

The collaborated team effort left little for me to do except take in each precious moment. The rehearsal had gone smoothly. Everything was in place for tomorrow. Yet as much as I was enjoying myself, an acute sadness lingered nearby, like the other side of a coin, inseparable from the joy of the occasion.

Friends and family members I couldn't imagine this event without filled the house. All except for one. The one person who, no matter how much my heart ached for him to be there, wasn't coming. The pain of missing Dad pulsed in every beat.

"Everything okay?" Riley's arms enclosed me in a shield of comfort.

"Yeah," I whispered. "Just a little caught up, I guess."

Riley glanced full circle around the packed living room. "I know what you mean. Do you want to take a—?"

"There you two are." Jaycee and Trevor pranced up from behind and prodded us toward the less crowded kitchen. "It's nearly impossible to catch you guys alone."

Riley and I shared an amused glance. Evidently, her interference didn't count.

"We want to give you our wedding present tonight, so we can see your faces when you open it." Jaycee looped her arm around Trevor's to keep herself from lifting off the ground in a bubble of excitement.

"A little something for the honeymoon." Trev's

mischievous tone launched a fleet of nerves trickling down my spine.

He handed the immaculately wrapped box to Riley, whose arms buckled under the unexpected weight. He slid it onto the countertop.

Jaycee raised on her toes, shoulders nearly touching her ears. "Em, you open it."

Gripping one edge of the box, I motioned to Riley for a joint effort. We opened the flaps together. My stunned gaze bounced from Riley to Jaycee to Trevor. "You bought us chai?"

"An endless supply." Trevor elbowed Riley in the arm. "I know they have all that daylight in Alaska, but we thought you could use a little caffeine too. Trust me. You're not going to want to sleep."

Riley scratched his jawbone. "Wow, um, thanks, Trev."

Heat claimed my cheeks. My eyes widened at Jaycee, but she only laughed. "I told you to wait until it was your turn."

Trevor hooked an arm around her. "C'mon, babe. Let's give these two a few minutes alone to let it sink in that they're actually getting married tomorrow."

They fled the kitchen, and Riley rubbed his chin with the back of his hand. "Nothing like a little humor to defuse the tension."

"Is that what just happened?" I hunched against the counter.

He set his hands around either side of me, hemming

me in his arms. "You're very cute when you're embarrassed."

I strained not to give in to his lopsided grin. "Really?"

"Mm-hmm." He bent forward until his lips barely brushed mine. "Almost as cute as when you're angry."

With the distance between us lost, my pulse skyrocketed.

"Ahem." Austin fake coughed. "Sorry to interrupt."

Liar.

"But I need to borrow the groom for a few minutes."

Riley looked at me but didn't budge until I nodded.

Left in the empty kitchen, I ran my hands along my arms. I probably should've rejoined the rest of the party in the living room. But now that I had a few minutes alone, I knew exactly where I wanted to go.

I managed to slip out the back door unnoticed. A wave of solitude followed me down the stairs and into the quiet backyard, where I settled on the cool sand bordering the water's edge.

Here I was again—under the stars in the same place I'd come to clear my head ever since I was a child. Even when I hadn't fully understood what I was searching for, sitting by the lake had felt like being home. Peaceful. Uncomplicated. Life had always made sense here.

A gentle breeze from across the lake covered me in a welcome-back embrace. The trees bordering the small inlet beside my uncle's property waved shadows over the shoreline. I closed my eyes and hugged my knees to my chest, soaking it all in.

It would've been nice to take our Alaskan honeymoon in the winter when the Northern Lights were their most stunning, but the stars here at the lake had to come close to matching their beauty.

"Thought I might find you out here." Mom crossed the yard, sat beside me, and pressed a freckled arm against mine. "All those summers here, I'd be going crazy wondering where you were, but your dad somehow always knew." She laughed softly at the memories. "He wouldn't let me go after you either. Said you'd come back in when you were good and ready."

"Sometimes I think he understood me better than I understood myself."

"He had a way of seeing things others weren't able to. It's one of the many reasons why I fell in love with him."

I turned to her, emotions churning. "I miss him so much."

"Oh, honey. I miss him too." She cradled my head to her shoulder and stroked my hair the way she'd done since I was a kid.

Mom leaned back and dabbed the skin under her eyes, finding a strength I wasn't used to seeing in her. "Knowing he'd miss your wedding day was one of the hardest things he had to come to terms with." She withdrew a small envelope from her pocket. "But he made sure he'd still be here for you, sweetheart. He wanted you to have this tomorrow."

I stared at the letter in my hands and swallowed hard.

"I thought maybe you'd want to read it tonight instead."

I hugged her again and held on as tightly as I held on to Dad's memory. "Thanks, Mom. I love you."

"I love you too." She squeezed my hand, rose to her feet, and wiped the sand off her pants. "I'll give you some time alone."

Time alone with Dad. I couldn't have asked for anything more.

She stopped at the bottom of the steps leading to the second story deck. "And Emma? Don't stay out too late. Jaycee will have my head if you have bags under your eyes tomorrow morning." Her soft laughter followed her up the wooden staircase. She knew Jaycee so well.

In the quiet, the heavens cast a glow over the lake. I used to stare at the sky and imagine the world as a brilliant painting. I'd sit on the edge of the shore, waiting for any hint of what the next paint stroke would be.

Had Dad known all along that I'd end up here on the eve of my wedding day? Had he known what it would take for me to reach this point?

Drawing in a breath, I opened the letter. His handwriting reached off the page into the memory of his voice.

Emma, what I'd give to see my baby girl on her wedding day. I've never been angry at God for the things I don't understand. But knowing I won't be there to give you away was too much to bear until I understood I don't have to miss it. Not really. If I close my eyes, I can envision the day perfectly.

There you are—white dress, hair dolled up, looking as stunning as your mother did the day I married her. I'm beside you, prouder than any father could be. Austin's up front, your biggest fan. And your mom's already demolished an entire box of tissues.

But you, my compassionate, headstrong daughter, steal the show. It's hard to miss the way the groom's eyes light up as we make our way to the altar. He loves you. There's no question in my mind you've made the right choice. So, with slightly more ease, knowing you'll be well taken care of, your mother and I release you into the wonderful journey of marriage.

There's so much I wish I could tell you, advice I wish I had the time to give. But none more important than this: never stop growing a love between you that always protects, always trusts, always hopes, and always perseveres. It's that kind of love, Emma, that'll never fail.

No tears of sorrow today, kiddo. Give Austin a good rib cage shot for me if he slacks on his job of walking you down the aisle. And be sure to tell that good-looking mom of yours how breathtaking she is.

Congratulations, honey. I'm so sorry I can't be there in person, but please know how very much I love you. More than words can express.

With all my love, today and always,

Dad

No tears? Was he kidding? Mom was right. There was no way I could've handled reading his letter tomorrow. I clutched the paper to my chest and held on to the part of him my heart didn't have to let go of. Ever.

282 | CRYSTAL WALTON

Something jingled behind me, followed by Jake's wet nose sliding under my arm. He collapsed beside me and rested his head on my thigh. Animals always knew when you needed them most.

"Not getting cold feet, are you?" Riley called from the bottom of the stairs.

Apparently, my half-hearted smile wasn't convincing enough to override the tear marks left on my cheeks. Riley was at my side in a heartbeat.

"What's wrong? Is everything okay?"

I handed him the letter, not ready to speak.

One look at the signature was all it took. Riley's eyes filled with a yearning to take all my pain on himself. He hugged me to his side in an enclosure of steady comfort. The kind that clothed me in the truth of every word Dad had just shared with me. Riley was, and always would be, my evidence that some dreams were worth never giving up on.

Jake wandered back under the porch, and Riley and I stayed on the shore. A breeze whispered across the lake. Each time the water rippled into the shoreline, minutes drifted a little closer to all we'd been waiting for.

Reaching this point hadn't handed me a blueprint. I didn't know where our home in Nashville would be, how opening a center there would play out, or what traveling with Riley would look like. After everything I'd gone through the last couple of years, I still had questions. Even some regrets. But in the very place I'd always gone to look for answers, I sat now, holding on to the only one I needed.

The earlier bustle inside the house had fizzled out completely by the time we headed back in. A bright yellow sticky note greeted us at the sliding door with a message written in very distinct Jaycee-handwriting: *Eye mask in freezer!*

Riley and I looked from the note to each other and laughed. I shouldn't have been the least bit surprised Jaycee would know I'd been crying, or that she'd already prepared a remedy.

Eye mask in hand, I tiptoed behind Riley down the quiet hallway toward my bedroom on the backside of the house. We lingered in the doorway. A faint streak of moonlight trickled through the window and highlighted a look in Riley's eyes that defined everything words couldn't. My fingers grazed down the front of his T-shirt in search of a way to say good night.

Riley stared at the hardwood floor. "You remember the night we were talking outside your apartment when Jaycee came to pick you up? I never got to finish telling you how I knew nothing would stop me from marrying you."

I leaned against the trim.

"When we first met, you asked me if I'd ever thought about pursuing a career as a recording artist, and I told you I did once. A long time ago."

A clear remembrance of that day in his apartment came to mind.

"There's more to that story than I first told you." He kept his voice even, but I sensed a twinge of uneasiness.

"I reached a breaking point the summer before I left for school. An all-day fight with my dad ended in him storming off, disappearing for hours in some bar. He came home that night angry at the world. Got into it with my mom the second he stepped foot into the kitchen. He didn't know I was out back on the deck, overhearing every word."

Riley tilted his head against the jamb. "I'd tried so hard not to be a disappointment to him. But after that night, I was done. Done trying to please him. Done with music. With hoping things would change. I busted my guitar in half and ran off to that park where we found Jasmine. I could shut everything else out there, you know?" He shook his head. "But not that night."

A deep breath broadened his shoulders. "I stood on the edge of that cave and buried my identity as a musician. Said I'd never dream again." He met my eyes with honest vulnerability. "Right after, I swore someone said, '*Yes, you will.*'"

Riley kneaded his neck. "I know that sounds crazy. I was the only one out there. Believe me. I checked to make sure." He laughed but then sobered. "Crazy or not, the only thing I kept thinking was, how? Dreams are too painful."

His forehead creased as he stared at the floor again. "I'll never be able to explain this, but I saw a vision of a girl. She didn't have a name. I couldn't make out any features except the way she looked at me. With such belief, it negated every doubt I'd ever had about myself." A long blink lifted his lashes. "And right then, I knew, this girl—whoever she was—was going to help me find the hope to dream again."

I wrung the eye mask and fought down more tears.

Riley's fingers found mine. He led me toward the twin bed along the back wall, lifted the covers over top of my legs, and sat beside me. "I convinced myself I'd imagined the whole thing," he continued. "Until I saw you for the first time on campus that day. You remember?"

Did he really have to ask?

He smiled without missing a beat. "Those eyes. When I saw you again at Nuts and Jolts, I had to meet you. Had to know." Starlight peered in behind him. "I kept telling myself I was crazy. But the more time we spent together, the more I couldn't fight it."

I brushed my hand over top of his, voice lost.

He inhaled. "That day in the woods after you told me about your dreams and the way you'd been hurt, I went home furious. How could God use you to restore hope in my life but leave me helpless to do the same for you?"

Faint traces of the pain he'd felt then colored his eyes now. "I couldn't sleep that night. I sat straight up in bed and demanded an answer. And just like that time at the cave, I heard a response: 'Because it's something only I can do.'"

Riley outlined the edges of my sapphire ring with his

fingertip. "So, I made a promise that night. I'd let you go. But if God ever brought you back to me, I never would again."

He lifted my hand to his lips, lowered it back to the sheet, and looked at me with the same assurance that'd kept him grounded since the beginning.

Had God really been leading us to each other from before we even met? All this time. All the prayers that had felt unanswered. All the delays, the questions, the doubts. He'd been working out His plan through it all.

My lashes creased together in awe and gratefulness. I held on to Riley's hand, overwhelmed by the extent God would go to show His love for us, even more so by the hope tied inseparably to grace.

"You know," I said once I found my voice again. "Sometimes I think about how much easier the road could've been if we knew the things we know now, but honestly? I wouldn't trade any of it." Not after seeing how purpose had flowed through every step. Even through the pain.

"Does that mean you're ready for tomorrow?"

"The beginning of always?" I smiled. "Definitely."

Riley's grin slanted. "Forever's kind of a long time. Think you'll still love me when I keep you up 'til two in the morning playing the piano?"

"Hmm." I squinted and scrunched my lips to the side. "Only if you'll still love me when all I make you for dinner are frozen meals."

Riley shook the bed with laughter. "Deal." He leaned in to kiss me, crossed the room, and stopped in the doorway. "This is the last night I have to say goodbye."

For that reason alone, tomorrow couldn't come fast enough.

ALL ALONG

I DREW BACK the curtains and absorbed the colors of a new day rushing in. It wasn't the first time I'd woken up to a sunrise, but today was different. Today, the sunlight filled the room like a faithful friend offering a gift it had been bursting at the seams to give me.

Outside my window, rows of rustic oak chairs, separated by a single aisle down the middle, lined the beach just beyond where the grass transitioned into the shoreline. Jaycee had obligingly set the scene for no more than a hundred people, to keep the ceremony small and intimate and perfect.

I sat on the sill—eyes closed, bathed in warmth—and simply breathed.

Jaycee screeched to a stop across the room. "You're not in the shower yet?"

I tried not to laugh at her militant pose. "Is it okay if I wash my hair all by myself?"

She tapped her imaginary watch. "That depends."

I saluted my commanding officer and marched straight for the bathroom. Steam blanketed around me. But, for once, I didn't need its calming effect. It didn't matter what length I had to go to to get ready. It didn't matter how many stairs I had to climb down in my dress or how many pairs of eyes would be glued on me as I walked down the aisle. Nothing could interfere with the joy consuming me today.

Jaycee got to work on me the second I emerged from the bathroom. What would've taken me days to accomplish only took her a mere two hours. Before I knew it, I was standing in the middle of the bedroom, surrounded by the glistening eyes of my mom, aunt, soon-to-be mother-in-law, and my best friend.

Simple, yet elegant. That was the goal, and Jaycee had pulled it off magnificently, including the dress. Aside from the lace embellishments along the straps and a thin border garnishing the neckline, a simple satin layer coated my body in a floor-length, A-line fit. And the best part was, I didn't have to wear heels.

Mom covered her mouth. "Oh, sweetheart."

"No crying before the ceremony." Jaycee fluttered her fingers in front of her own eyes. "Okay, ladies, it's time for everyone to take their places."

She squeezed my hands and offered a final proud smile at her work of art before flitting off to join the rest of the wedding party. The door that had turned into a revolving turntable all morning now stood still.

In front of an oversized mirror, I straightened out the single pearl on the necklace Dad had given me all those years ago. For the slightest moment, I thought I saw him standing beside me with a smile that held my heart. "I love you, Daddy."

A knock at the door rippled over my shoulders. "The prince kindly requests an audience with the..." Austin stopped halfway through the door, staring as though he didn't recognize me. "...Princess," he finished slowly.

I looked down at my dress. "What?"

He shook his head, for perhaps the first time in his life, speechless. Smiling, he extended his arm to me. "Your chariot awaits, my lady."

I took his arm and poked him in the side. "Yards of satin fabric, and I can still take you down."

"You wish," he said from the corner of his mouth. "I think you should just concentrate on making it down those steps without tripping."

I gripped his sleeve. "What do you think *you're* here for?"

"Really? 'Cause I was planning on leaning on *you*." He cocked his chin. "You know. The whole bum leg thing."

I gave him that rib shot Dad had mentioned in his letter.

Austin laughed but covered my hand on his arm and looked at me with the same tenderness Dad would've if he were there. "Don't worry, Em. I won't let you fall."

I batted away the tears Jaycee would've killed me for

shedding before we'd made it through pictures. We rounded the corner into the dining room where Jasmine swayed in front of the sliding glass door. Wearing an iridescent flower girl dress and tiny butterfly barrettes to match a darling necklace, she couldn't have looked more precious. Lost in a fairy tale of glass slippers, she dangled her clear shoe on the tip of her foot at different angles in the sunlight.

Austin cleared his throat.

She dropped her shoe and ran straight for us. "Emma!"

Austin intercepted her right in time. "I'm sorry," he said in a stellar robot impersonation. "You've just entered a no-touching zone. All hugs are reserved for after the ceremony."

He offered an apologetic shrug when I glared at him. "Jaycee's orders."

Of course.

I twirled Jasmine around by the hand to showcase her dress. "Great pick."

Eyes sparking, she returned my wink.

"You're up, kiddo." Austin pointed at the door and the processional already underway.

A silent squeal spread across every inch of her little face as she spun and raced for the door. She stole a minute to smooth out her hair before counting her steps onto the deck.

I leaned over to Austin. "I think she might steal the show."

He laughed in full agreement and offered his arm again.

Outside, a gentle breeze carrying the scent of fresh flowers swirled around the edges of my hair, danced across my bare shoulders, and flittered to the opposite side of the deck.

"Ready?" Austin whispered.

Like never before. I lifted the hem of my dress off the ground, and he kept me close on the way down the stairs.

Behind the stretch of chairs, Melody manned a makeshift soundboard. She'd exchanged her miniature earbuds for a much larger headset. Everything about the context fit her perfectly.

Rows filled with smiling faces and tear-stained cheeks bordered the shoreline as music cued our turn down the aisle. I recognized the song Melody had chosen as the one Riley had been working on when I'd visited him in Nashville. Except in this rendition, the elegant resonance of violins complemented the piano's rich tenor.

Friends and family all rose to their feet. I tightened my fingers around Austin's sleeve again. With more poise than I'd ever seen from him, he led me along the sandy path toward a simple arbor where Riley waited for me.

In front of Jaycee, Jasmine clicked her heels together in a twitch of visible excitement. Riley's dad stood by his side, tall and proud.

Halfway down the aisle, I flashed a peek at my bare feet beneath the bottom of my dress. Riley laughed with his eyes and beamed at me the exact way Dad said he would.

When we reached the front, he tore his gaze from mine long enough to nod at Austin.

Austin kissed my cheek and sat in the front row beside Mom, who immediately took my place latching on to his arm for stability.

I transferred my bouquet to Jaycee and joined hands with Riley. For the slightest second, I worried we should've asked the pastor to prompt our vows for us. But as soon as I heard Riley's voice, everything else dissolved. Right then, it was only him and me.

"I, Riley Preston, take you, Emma Matthews, to be my wife. I promise to love you faithfully, to stand by your side through the certainty of today and the questions of tomorrow, and to sing you home if you ever lose your way. I promise to protect your heart, share your hopes and dreams, and cherish you as my best friend each and every day for as long as we both shall live."

His eyes, as clear blue as the water beside us, gleamed with the fullness of his promise. After everything we'd gone through—all the ways we'd grown—it was a promise I was confident I could finally offer him in return.

"I, Emma Matthews, take you, Riley Preston, to be my husband. I promise to spend every day learning to love you through the best and worst of what's to come. I promise never to let you lose sight of who you are or doubt who you're becoming. I promise to honor and respect you, comfort and support you, and love and cherish you without condition. From this day forward, I unite my heart, my dreams, my life with yours for as long as we both shall live."

With the sacred vow of exchanged rings and a kiss that, thanks to Trevor, solicited enough whoops from the audience to make me blush, the ceremony ended.

Announced as Mr. and Mrs. Preston for the first time, Riley and I ran down the center aisle under a shower of birdseed, holding on to everything we'd thought had been out of reach. All the broken pieces of the past came together. There was no rewinding time, only looking forward with an unyielding certainty that the best was yet to come.

———

IF I EVER HAD ANY doubt whatsoever about Jaycee becoming a wedding planner, it vanished the second we crossed the threshold leading to the outdoor reception.

A series of white and fuchsia magnolia trees fenced in a field along Lake Tahoe's stunning backdrop. Green branches with clusters of purple blooms wept like open umbrellas over the path ushering us toward a sheer canopy tent.

Strings of lights hung from intertwined tree branches stretched across the enchanting ceiling above tables decorated with Jaycee's artistic touch. I clung to Riley's side, overwhelmed by how magical it all seemed.

I'd doubted anything could've surpassed the feeling of sharing our vows. But here in this picture of elegance, my heart told me this was only the beginning.

From toasts, to dinner, to dessert, Jaycee had arranged the flow of the evening to match the soft ambience perfectly.

While waiters made subsequent rounds across the floor, Austin slipped up to the front of the tent and tapped the microphone. "Excuse me, everyone."

The hum of conversations transitioned into an expectant silence with every eye fixed on him.

Except mine.

I studied the mischievous grin Riley was failing to hide.

He leaned over. "Remember that surprise I was telling you about?" He kissed the bottom of my ear, pushed his chair back, and hustled up to the corner of the stage.

Austin tilted the microphone to the side and cleared his throat. I wasn't used to seeing him nervous. That wasn't a good sign. I stole a glance at Mom across several tables. Her eyes flitted in my direction, but she looked just as surprised.

"Hi, everyone," Austin started again. "For those of you I haven't met yet, I'm Emma's brother, Austin. I think most of you know our dad can't be here today."

The quiver in his voice at the mention of Dad almost

single-handedly unraveled the threads keeping the pain of missing him at bay.

"But long before Emma was old enough to even start thinking about marriage, he was already picturing this day. He had a way of trusting how things were going to turn out."

A collective sigh rang across the tent.

"There's a special bond between a father and his son, but there's nothing quite like the love a dad has for his little girl."

Austin turned my way, focusing his words to me directly. "Dad asked me to give you his wedding present today."

He strode to the corner of the stage, strapped our dad's acoustic guitar over his shoulder, and returned to the microphone.

My heart stopped at the beginning of the song Dad had played for me a myriad of times throughout my life. I'd fallen asleep in his lap to that tender sound of strings. I'd watched from the border of the kitchen, listening in as he wrote the chords in his study. Even now, I still heard him humming along as Austin played.

When I'd asked him once to sing the words, he had simply smiled. "*Songs are like stories,*" he'd said. "*When we open up our hearts to dream, the story writes the lyrics.*" He'd laughed at the puzzled look on my face and then knelt until we were eye to eye. "*Keep dreaming, Emma. And your story will write lyrics even more beautiful than the music.*"

The memory raced for my tear ducts and blurred Austin on the stage.

"Dad worked on this song for a lot of years. He left it unfinished, but not because he ran out of time. He left the ending for someone else."

Riley joined Austin at the front of the stage with his guitar in hand.

"Dad made me promise to give you this song as his wedding gift with the one condition that your husband helps me sing it."

Austin stumbled over the word "husband." No one else probably noticed the inflection, but I was thankful for a much-needed chuckle.

With Riley strumming alongside him, Austin faced the audience. "The song's called, 'All Along.'"

The music began as it always had. I gripped my napkin in my lap, unsure I was ready to hear the lyrics for the first time.

"A blank canvas, a new song. A little girl searching for where she belongs. With a thirst for life, she laughs and twirls, a smile to share, a heart unfurled."

Riley stepped up to his own microphone. "A blank canvas, a new melody. A little boy searching for who he's meant to be. Villains and heroes, lassoes and swords, a make-believe world ready to explore."

They harmonized together. "A dance through life, day by day, to the music in your heart, guiding your way. Moments strung together in an incomplete song, leading to the one who's been singing with you all along."

Jaycee took my hand captive under the table.

Austin adjusted the microphone. "A stroke of paint, a new verse sung. A young woman's heart is left undone. Questions stirred, seasons changed. Hope holds on, dreams remain."

Riley's fingers danced over the strings, his voice one with the words. "A stroke of paint, a new chord played. A young man's fears ready to trade, for a faith unshaken and courage unseen. He steps forward, daring to believe."

They sang the chorus together again, and the music reached past the finite borders around us.

"Dreams collide, hope defined. Meaning of love found in their eyes. As life unfolds, a new story's told. A song begun, now sung as one."

As Riley and Austin both strummed the ending to the most precious gift Dad could've given me, Austin's gaze found mine once more. "With love, from Dad."

Jaycee released my hand. Hearing the story of our lives sung to the same melody I'd always connected to my love for Dad left too many tears to stifle. I fixed my eyes on Riley. I might not have known how life would write the remainder of our story, but this much I knew without question. The song in our hearts would lead the way.

The rest of the Prestons joined Riley on the stage and each picked up an instrument while couples moseyed onto the dance floor.

Austin hopped off and cut through the crowd to my

table. Flashing his familiar grin, he extended a hand. "May I have this dance?"

I circled around the table and joined him on the floor.

He drew me into a dancing frame. "Singing that song wasn't the only promise I made Dad."

I leaned back and searched my brother's eyes.

"I promised him I'd look after you the way he would've. Promised I'd be there to listen or offer advice. Protect you without interfering with the things you had to learn on your own." He laughed. "It wasn't always easy."

I tugged on the back of his hair, trying not to laugh too.

"Today," Austin said, sincerity filling his voice again. "I'm transferring that role to Riley."

I understood what he was saying, but I'd never stop needing him in my life. "I might be married now, but I'll always be your little sister."

His smile joined mine.

Someone from behind Austin tapped his shoulder. "Mind if I cut in?"

"A. J.?" Even though we'd had a small gathering, I hadn't seen him in the crowd of faces.

Austin bowed his head at A. J., winked at me, and invited Mom to join him on the floor instead.

I stared at the grass, but A. J. didn't permit much time to linger. He held out a hand. "You proved me wrong,

Em. You're even more beautiful than I'd imagined you'd be."

I fluttered off his charm as he drew me into a dancing hold. "Glad to know some things never change."

He laughed but then tilted his head, as though something wasn't quite right. "No heels?"

I lifted on my toes to fit in his arms the way I had at Jaycee's wedding.

"Better." His grin crept up the side of his cheek. "You know, we're kinda experts at this whole dancing thing." He leaned in to whisper. "We could really show these people up. For the record."

I laughed, then set my chin on his shoulder. "*For the record*, it means a lot to me that you're here. I was worried you wouldn't come."

"You kidding? I wouldn't have missed it." A. J. spun me around and drew me back in. And for a long, unspoken moment, we both held on to a friendship we'd never forget.

He rested his cheek against my hair. "I'm really happy for you, Em."

I clung to his shoulder. "I've always wanted you to find this same happiness."

"I know," he whispered. "And you've given me the hope to believe one day I will."

I leaned back to face him, but he had his eyes closed.

"Life's meant to be lived with your eyes wide open, remember?" I said, repeating the same thing he'd spoken to me on another occasion, on another dance floor. "Promise me, A. J."

He lifted his fingers in the air in his notorious Boy Scout salute. "I promise."

His gaze flickered past me. Smiling, he took one of my hands and twirled me around again, this time letting go.

I spun right into Riley's arms.

"Congratulations," A. J. said to him. "I'm happy for you both."

Riley bowed, graciously extending A. J. the respect he'd earned.

A. J. looked from Riley to me. His eyes didn't hold any trace of hidden pain. No sorrow or regret. Only sincerity from a friend who wanted the best for me.

With a final smile I'd always remember, A. J. turned to follow a path that would lead him to his own story.

Riley closed me in his arms from behind. "He's found courage he didn't know he had."

"I think we all have." Thanks to grace. That was the thing about love. It didn't wait for us to have it all together or give up on us when anyone in their right mind would've. It didn't wait for us to come running in desperation or turn its back even when we turned ours. It pursued us first. From the beginning, through every-thing, without fail.

There had been times in my life when I'd experienced that kind of love—in glimpses, outpourings. But standing here now, I sank into a truth that had accompanied that love all along. "It's easier to hope for something when you finally understand it's worth waiting for."

Riley's smile brushed against my hair. He turned me to him, keeping me close. As many times as I'd listened to his voice dance with music, this moment would forever be my favorite.

The reception carried on around us. We could've been surrounded by a thousand people or merely ten. It didn't matter. Right then, the lights dimmed to only candlelight. The piano and violins' soft cadence waned in the background. Faces in the crowd faded out of focus. And time—once an enemy, now a friend—slowed until it felt like we were the only ones there.

Riley leaned back from a kiss and kept his fingers under my ear. No words. Just the promise of never letting go. After all this time, his eyes still anchored me, as they would every day we danced throughout our small part of always.

ABOUT THE AUTHOR

Crystal received her Bachelor of Arts from Messiah College in PA, married her exact opposite in upstate NY, and earned her Master of Arts from Regent University in VA, where she currently resides with her husband and two sons. Crystal writes contemporary clean and inspirational romances fueled by venti green teas. She'd love to connect with you at crystal-walton.com and Facebook.

ACKNOWLEDGMENTS

Dave, thanks for cheering me to press through a race I've questioned over and over again whether I have the strength to run. I'm so glad to have you as my dance partner throughout our own small part of always.

Jessica and Erynn, when I first started, I never imagined I'd be blessed with such a tremendous pair of editors. Thank you for the priceless ways you've sown into this series and into my growth as an author. Your investment has filled an uphill journey with laughs and tears that've kept me pushing forward. And it simply wouldn't be right ending it all without saying . . . Team A. J.!

Shaela, thank you for creating such brilliant covers. I couldn't love them more.

Mom, I've always treasured you as the prayer warrior and cheerleader for your family. Your commitment to standing alongside me through this venture has been perhaps the most beautiful depiction of why.

To each member of my launch team, thanks for the many ways you've rallied behind this series. Your prayers and support have been my baseline. Thank you.

To each of my readers, I may not know you personally, but I've prayed for you. From before I released the first book, you've been on my heart. Thank you for giving this series a try, for letting these characters share in a small part of your life, and for joining me along a journey of faith, courage, and hope. Keep going.